# From Seven to the Sea

*For Kanayo Sugiyama*

# From Seven to the Sea

## Jayne Joso

Seren is the book imprint of
Poetry Wales Press Ltd
57 Nolton Street, Bridgend, Wales, CF31 3AE
www.serenbooks.com
Facebook: facebook.com/SerenBooks
Twitter: @SerenBooks

ISBNs
Paperback – 978-1-78172-482-8
Ebook – 978-1-78172-483-5
Kindle – 978-1-78172-484-2

A CIP record for this title is available from the British Library.

The publisher acknowledges the financial assistance of the Welsh
Books Council.

Cover photograph: Nine Köpfer on Unsplash

Author photograph: Natacha Horn

Printed in Bembo by Latimer Trend and Company Ltd, Plymouth.

# From Seven to the Sea

# 1

Seven, thought Esther, I am going to be seven. It seemed to be a significant number, perhaps more important than any that had gone before.

On a beautiful summer's morning, when the sun came bright, the events of the day about to unfold, unfold and render themselves crystalline, Esther turned seven. And what might never be debated was the certainty that this very particular day would carve itself deep as landmark; and, like a paper doll, Esther would part from the flimsy perforations at the edges, the tiny slithers of paper that had held her in place, and slip from the page with the breeze.

It was already proving to be an especially busy day. Lots of adults that were not usually there, dashing from room to room, and all of them dressed up. Was all of this for her birthday? She went to ask, but no one stopped, and she didn't mind, somehow the bustle only added to the feeling of birthday bliss. Things were being gathered up in a rush of excitement, packed into suitcases and boxes, and carried out to cars and a huge old van. It wasn't obvious how any of this related to her special day, but she didn't give it too much thought. It would all become clear. So, when another adult hurtled past and missed her question yet again, she gave a cheerful shrug and smiled. There'd be presents later, and perhaps quite a lot. So many people; she skipped back up the stairs as it suddenly occurred to her to make sure that she was ready, get out of pyjamas and put on a dress. But as soon as she had done this, struggling with the buttons, Mum and a cluster of other grown-up women barged into her room. They were in a terrible hurry, no one had dressed her! Esther pulled out the skirt of the dress she was in, and laughed, she already had on this one!

Esther hadn't realised that her mum was re-marrying. No one had told her, or perhaps each thought someone else had told her. Still, when she found herself suddenly and efficiently undressed, then zipped and buttoned into another dress, a bridesmaid dress, it seemed quite clear. There was a wedding. Whose? Your mum's. Your mother's. She's marrying that man. That one, that one over there...

He stood in the doorway. Esther vaguely recollected having seen him before. But more from the side, and from the back, as he walked away. Apparently, he had bought her a small doll some weeks before, though he had not spoken to the little girl, and had not actually given it to her himself. Didn't she remember? The little doll with the bendy joints, brown skin, the yellow hair? Mum had passed it to her, and at the time it had not been at all clear who the doll was from. Was it then, from him? Truly?

Esther looked him over now, since opportunity presented itself. She felt awed by the idea of the wedding, and quietly excited. She had to stand very still as the women brushed and twirled her hair and added in things that scratched the scalp, small flower decorations she later discovered—they matched the blue dress they'd put her in.—If Mum was to marry, then… well then, then she'd have a dad. Wow! …and, *wow!* She'd never known her own. 'A dad', she repeated silently to herself, 'Father', '*my* father…' tumbling the syllables around her mouth. The idea suddenly a tiny seed and full of promise. This was her chance then, the chance to have one. Brilliant! And there was every possibility that it was going to be even more brilliant since the whole thing was all so new. Her thoughts ran on, each colliding with the one ahead, forcing out the ever more pleasing 'father, daughter' story. She felt warm, and she felt proud. And how proud he might be of her! If things went well. If she did things well. If she was good and kind. And polite and fun. She would show him her drawings – the really good ones. And she would listen carefully and learn from him.

As the women finished dressing her, the man spoke directly to her mother. He did this over the little girl's head, quite as though she wasn't there, quite as though no one else was there. He used her mother's name in a somewhat exasperated tone, 'Maud…' he said, '*Maud*, we really have to get going.'

'We're almost ready,' Maud replied. The women seemed intent on taking care of the socks, and buckles on sandals too, so with each of her hands resting on the shoulders of the crouched down women, Esther took advantage of the moment for a further stolen and prolonged perusal of the man. He was not very tall, and he didn't have a nice face. His nose was small and plump, and round and red, but his eyes were quite a pretty blue. He didn't have a mouth, just a line, like a cut, with shorter, thinner lines travelling upwards towards his nose, scratches in a rock wall. And when the jaws parted, just inside the line, lay thick yellow teeth, dinosaur teeth, the kind you see in museums. He was old, Esther decided, or quite old, but that was alright, Mum was old, or fairly old – and this was discovered following claims of 'twenty-one' some three years running. In fact, Mum was fifty-five, the age of her school friends' grandmas— Esther finally settled that the lower half of the man's face wasn't very nice at all. But it was good at least that he had pretty, blue eyes. They looked a bit smiley.

# 2

It was a long car ride to the ceremony. So many bumpy roads. The sun's hotness burned through the windows as yet another corner was taken badly, the driver, the groom, attempting to cover it over with jocular remarks about it being very difficult to navigate such tricky mountain roads, always worse so close to sea, *like a chicane!* He laughed. Esther slid back and forth across the back seat. Shiny mock leather. It had a funny smell and was sticky and hot to the touch. The windows were all tight shut, and leaving it too long she couldn't catch her breath for quite long enough to ask if perhaps they might be opened. Disorientated, and by now made somewhat anxious by the day's surprise events, she found herself hiccupping, and this with greater and greater rapidity, until, in a final sudden spasm, and a *humorous* jerk of the wheel, she vomited down the special bridesmaid dress.

It was hot. It was humid. They couldn't waste time pulling over, and there clearly wasn't space to do so. Not safe at all. No designated spots for such things. There were tissues in the glovebox. Maud, by some feat of acrobatics, cleaned Esther up as best she could whilst leaning over the front seat and into the back. No, there wasn't any water that the child could rinse her mouth with, and no, it still wasn't possible to stop. If you stopped, it would be difficult and dangerous to pull out again onto the road, very poor visibility thereabouts; besides, and as had already been pointed out, it would make them late.

The car stank. Esther stank, and hiccupped. After informing Esther that she should sit still and try to keep herself calm and quiet, the driver and front seat passenger made the remainder of the journey in silence. The little girl gripped the car seat with her hands under her knees as best she could, emitting only the occasional nervous burp which, after the first few, began to make her giggle. The man surveyed her in the rear-view mirror. Esther looked down at her dangling feet. She needed a wee.

# 3

On arrival, it turned out that you couldn't be a bridesmaid with sick all down your dress, and Esther was quickly bundled into a plainer summer dress that her mum had packed as spare—did she know that this might happen?—The man that Maud was marrying speculated that the spare dress was perhaps not smart enough to appear at the wedding ceremony itself, and it was perfectly possible that the child would vomit again. Esther was affronted by this, but didn't let him see. Maud hurried away, anxious to greet some guests arriving early. Esther viewed her in the distance.

In place of the wedding ceremony, it was decided that Esther would be taken to the beach. And those offering to do this were a nice middle-aged couple, old friends of Maud's from way back, Anne and Paul, generous guests, happy to help. They'd catch up with everyone later at the reception. The groom explained what a torment it was to have a child along on such an auspicious occasion. And on top of that, a child that puked like that. Hideous. Anne, at first unusually stuck for words, said that taking little Esther wasn't a problem, and that they didn't mind forgoing the ceremony, not in the least. I mean, *not in the least!* They'd been at Maud's first wedding, and this second wedding, they felt, was something of an unnecessary add-on in their friend's life; and it wasn't as if they knew the man. This was their first time to meet him and they had taken it as remiss of Maud that this should be this case. And she ought to be more cautious didn't she, it wasn't as though Esther's father had hung around for long. Just a matter of months wasn't it, in the end? Why marry at all? Why in such a hurry? Maud was hardly a pregnant teenager, and it wasn't the bloody 1950's for Christ's sake. Paul coughed a fake cough, a signal for Anne to lower her voice.

The couple hadn't had children and they liked little Esther a lot. They rarely got to see her since her mum had moved them so far up country some twelve months before. No, it would suit them well to take her out, and then meet up with the wedding party later. Anne held Esther's hand tight. Had the groom anything else he wanted to add before they departed?

'No, no!' he offered in his jocular manner, 'saving myself for the speeches!'

Well, that might be for the best... Paul patted Anne's shoulder as they walked away. The groom was probably under a certain amount of stress. *Stress?* Well, a wedding can affect some people that way. Paul recalled having heard that somewhere. Though he was cautious enough to add that he might have got it wrong, since he didn't recollect having felt that way himself.

The couple drove Esther out to the island nearby. They had a convertible and let the top down so that they could all enjoy the wind in their hair. They had done some research in advance, thinking to make the most of the time away and stay on a day or two. They would take Esther to the most wonderful beach on the far side of the island. They'd read that the sand there was almost white. Esther pictured it, and hummed cheerfully to calm her excitement. Paul told her to give a yell if she felt poorly and they could easily stop, and Anne had some water and apple juice if she wanted any.

When they reached the island, it seemed it was even better than they expected, there were dunes! 'Bloody great sand dunes!' Paul yelled, '*Fan-bloody-tast-ic! Ye-haa!*' Hide and seek, and tag ensued. And rolling down slopes, and sand sledging of sorts. Esther's tummy lurched and grumbled a few times but she wasn't sick again, and the stomach growl made Paul and Esther chuckle. He patted her shoulder and made sure she wasn't simply being brave or polite. Then he burped to make her giggle. Anne shook her head but smiled, the right balance somehow.

# 4

Happily sunned and freckled, Esther arrived back at the garden and the reception, refreshed and full of life with her newly adoptive Aunty Anne and Uncle Paul. She skipped along behind them, in through the large walled enclosure letting the tall, heavy wooden gate swing back hard behind her.

'*The gate!*' called the man, now legally her stepfather, eyeing her tiny frame from afar. The fresh new father, now red-faced from drinking, from sunshine, from yelling from the cut in his face that now made an angry 'O', was the man she was soon told by her mother, quietly, but firmly, that it would be best to call, Dad.

Esther glanced back at the huge gate. it had closed cleanly, and everyone seemed to be inside, no harm done. Nothing untoward. She skipped forwards after Anne and Paul, smiling bright, still full of the fun of their beach walks, the air, the sea, and wanting to bring this back, to let it lap gently over them, over them all, and make them all happy. Mum had just got married! There was a party. A garden party. And the garden was like the one in a story she knew, a secret garden, and it had high stone walls like a castle, and there were lawns and trees and shrubs, plenty of curious hiding places, and places that would make super-brilliant dens. She skipped about at hip height to the grown-ups. So many people. Old faces, and new ones. She wanted to tell them about her beach escapade with Anne and Paul, but people were getting drunk by now, 'sozzled' as her grandmother would say, and it was hard to get their attention. Her grandmother wasn't at the wedding, and neither was her grandad. That was a shame, she thought. And now they lived so far away. Well, Esther hoped she'd get to see them soon. Perhaps Mum would take her for a visit, and they could take photos of the wedding to show them. The wedding and her birthday.

Speeches came and popping corks, and later everyone had cake. A four-tier wedding cake. Esther scouted about. There was wedding cake, that was clear, white icing, layered up high, a misshapen plastic couple grimaced at the top; but no, and no, and no, not there either... there wasn't a birthday cake. Or? Now what was *that*? No, just an over-sized and elaborate sort of pork pie, but perhaps there'd be one later, when they had some tea, or tomorrow. Mum wouldn't have forgotten. Esther settled to admiring the tiny roses iced like a trailing pathway from tier to tier on Mum's cake. Her wrist was tapped sharply as the man said she shouldn't have cake in case it made her puke again. Then he turned away to admire a lady's dress. Esther regarded him with disdain, taking squares of cheese and pineapple on sticks instead, and hovering a moment with one of the sticks close to his bottom. If he took one step back, he would be impaled. Just one tiny step. Her chest tightened and she withdrew the stick, suddenly uncomfortable at the thought.

The garden belonged to the man and the house belonged to the man. Esther and Mum were moving there to live. Moving from their home and into the man's house. And she would be allowed to play in the man's garden if she kept off the flower beds and boarders and didn't climb the trees, and made sure to treat the gate with due care. The last part of this was reiterated sharply.

Esther placed the cheese-and-pineapple stick collection in her pocket, taking a stray chunk of pineapple as she went. It was terribly hot all of a sudden, she thought to go inside and get a glass of water.

Entering the house, and unsure of where the kitchen might be, she quickly found herself in a room full of funny looking things. Masks, sticks, feathers, and huge *huge* shells. Gnarly and beautiful. Treasure of the sea. Smooth on the inside, cold to the touch. She held one to her ear, she knew this from her grandad, and with a whoosh came the sound of the sea. It rushed into her ear, a great wave! Again. Then coming to rest. She put the shell back carefully in its place. Walking further in her eyes ran along the smooth shiny backs of ebony carved elephants with ivory tusks. Lots of them, in different sizes. Arranged in order of height, big at the front, tiny elephant at the rear. And there were giraffes made of wood, a family of them too; and more masks, some carved, painted, embellished with straw and small white shells. Some of them were quite a size, high up on the wall, and most of them looked scary. She ran her hand over an ebony black elephant. It was cold and smooth and beautiful. So very beautiful. She smiled.

'*Stop that!*' Esther froze. '*Right away… you stop that, right, right away!*' the man's voice shot through her body from behind. 'You shouldn't be in here. And you're not to start touching things that aren't yours.' She had already pulled her hand away. She didn't speak, nor did she turn to look at him. 'Now, out of here!' he ordered.

She left the room, she let herself breathe, then thought to leave the idea of water just for now and went outside again to skip.

The man, it would transpire, had a long list of 'rules', a long list of 'dislikes'… things that caused him 'displeasure' and on top of this, a list of 'hates', 'a bloody long list' as Paul might say. The *hate list* included: *the* Irish, the Scots, and people from Liverpool; anyone Asian, Oriental or Black, and anyone from the Middle East, especially those with beards, for they were terrorists, every last one of them. But more than any of these, he hated on sight, and would come to detest, Esther, just turned seven.

# 5

Esther went to sleep that night in her new bedroom. It seemed rather nice, all pale blue. A small window with a big tree outside. Heavy, dark blue curtains, framing. A nice bedside cupboard close by that she thought to hide small secret things inside. The bed itself was higher than her last bed, but that was alright. But after she'd lain awake awhile waiting for Mum to come and say good night, she began to notice the sounds the house made, wooden doors heavy on their hinges, the wind whistling thinly through old window frames, uneven floor boards creaking as though they were being stepped upon. 'Mum?' she called out softly, 'Mum...'

But no one came. Esther watched the clock on the table by the window, and after a few more minutes passed, she slipped out of bed and trod quietly along a dark hallway to the room that Mum was in. At the door, she hovered, there were sounds. Rustling sounds, and odd sounds difficult to make sense of. She nudged the door very gently, the air smelt a wine sort of smell, a musty sort of smell, and the lights weren't on, and Mum wasn't sitting up reading. Esther withdrew unable to settle quite on all that had happened, and then her mind switched suddenly, remembering that today was still her birthday! She giggled as she hopped from step to step down the big stairs and into the rooms below. She had been so busy with other things, with Anne and Paul, with exploring the garden, and with feasting on the party food, she had entirely forgotten. She turned a large white painted door handle and entered what surely was the living room. She switched on a light. There they were, presents. Some open, some piled up expectantly. She read the labels. It seemed most likely that the presents for Mum and the man had got mixed in with hers. It took rather a lot of rummaging, but finally it was clear. Not a one. Then they were in another room, of course, and perhaps if she didn't look too hard for them they would suddenly appear. Mum used to say that, sometimes things turn up just when you stop looking.

She opened the door again onto the room with the elephants and giraffes, and undisturbed, turned on a small lamp and looked around some more. The lamp made shadows, and the moonlight through the window, more. High up, the masks, she now decided, were not really scary, just wooden, wooden-looking, and like grandparents, would look lovely and smiley when you smiled back up at them. She tried this, and in some cases, though arguably not all, some of the masks did begin to smile. Some of them had carved-out eyes, others were painted in, she followed their line of sight. Straight to the floor. Stripes. Black and dirty white, zebra stripes. She was standing on a zebra skin, a zebra's coat, a sort of rug. 'Oh!' she gasped, stepping back quickly out of respect and uttering a gentle 'Sorry, soooo sorry…' She knelt down and began to stroke it gently.

When she woke, she felt a shiver. She had slept on her belly, her left arm stretched out broad across her zebra friend, and she had grown quite cold. Her face was crinkled from laying on the carpet next to the animal skin. She rolled over and yawned and shivered again. The sun glinted in through the shutters making their own pale stripes on things. The masks looked down on her, but there didn't seem to be any bother, and they all seemed friendly enough in the morning light. Remembering that she'd been told, and brusquely so, that she wasn't to go into this room, she jumped up quick, waved Zebra and the masks goodbye, blew a kiss to the others, the elephants and giraffes and more, and hopped back up the stairs and to her bed.

# 6

She slept on, and this much later than usual. When she woke again it was quite abrupt, her inner clock mistakenly thinking that this would be a school day. She chuckled when she remembered it was still the holidays. Summertime and school was still out. An easy kind of happy. Nonetheless, it seemed odd that Mum hadn't woken her.

Downstairs there was a lot of activity. Esther hung over the balustrade. Mum was unwrapping the last of the gifts. The man was asking where she would like things putting. He had taken to calling her 'Dear.' Esther arrived downstairs with a dance move, singing softly 'Dear darling, please excuse my writing…' from a song she knew from television. She didn't know the other words, so swirled around, humming gently and then repeating the few that she remembered.

She swung around again and this time collided with the man.

'Watch what you're doing!'

Startled, Esther tried to smile the sorry that she meant to say, but he frowned it out of her and the words, might they have come, slipped away. Dissolving on the air. Then Mum joined in, but she wasn't angry, she was almost never angry, even when it might be a good idea to be.

'Esther, what are you up to?' she asked.

'I wondered…'

'Yes, pet?'

'Well… nothing…' she felt embarrassed and somewhat annoyed to be called 'pet' in front of the man, but it was done now.

'Oh, I know what it is!' came Mum again, 'The presents! Your presents Esther, from your school friends…'

'Left in the hall didn't you say? Or thereabouts,' the man offered flippantly, chin hardly parting from coffee cup.

*Thereabouts?* Esther wrinkled her brow at the casual lack of clear direction, then she looked to the door to race away to the hallway, the entranceway, or perhaps the room near the front door, for the presents might still be under something or perhaps in a box she hadn't yet seen – 'the room' settled now very firmly in her mind as 'Africa' – just now it fitted quite well with *thereabouts*. She paused at the kitchen door, only in the hope of more accurate or detailed information, but none seemed forthcoming, and then Mum jumped in, '*Oh no, no, no… I remember, I remember*, you said last night', she looked to her husband and then at Esther who wondered at the further delay, 'I am sorry, pet, but I think they got left in the hall… *at our old place*. I meant to go back for them…'

'A lot of little packages, that was it, wasn't it?' The man feigned concern, 'From school pals, yes… well, expect you might not see them again…' he guffawed at this. Mum frowned and attempted to finish her thought, '…in a bag in the hallway. We were in such a silly rush…'

The man butt in again, directing his words at Esther, 'You'll get new pals now Love, at your new school. And presents, I dare say… next time 'round…'

*Love*, had he actually called her that? And 'school'? *'New'* school…?

'But we could go back for them, surely?' Mum offered up.

'As I said,' the man continued, a withering glance shot at the little girl, followed by a smile as he bit into an apricot, and slavered, 'Next year, now, eh, Love.'

*Love? Again! Again? Eh, Love!! ??* Had he really, truly said that? Esther ran. From the room, from the house, from the garden, and she pulled at the big fat gate with all her might, gratified by the thick slam it made behind her, by the sense of the weight of the wind behind her pushing her on. Tears streamed heavy down her face, salt in the wind pricked her cheeks and she felt her heart and then her blood as it shot through her veins, adrenaline filled. A tiger in flight.

This period of change in her life, though only the duration of one short summer, and perhaps the briefest step into autumn, would prove to be one that challenged a little girl and her sunshine spirit, quite beyond measure.

# 7

Left at the scene, Maud attempted to assert that it was important to return and collect her little girl's gifts. Would it really hurt to go back for them? The man made the pretence of having had the intention to do so, absolutely, and that he had only been 'teasing' and suggested that perhaps they might even make a day of it. That sound good? Splendid!

And so, 'Well… when then? *When?'* urged Maud. But he wasn't accustomed to being pinned down like this. Put on the spot.

'Let's see now, soon Dear, soon. We'll give it some thought.'

And too easily appeased, Maud had let it go. It might have gone some way in her relationship with her daughter, if somehow Esther had known that her mother had tried once more to get the presents back… tried to assert herself.

Outside the garden, with the gate onto that world tight shut, Esther carried on running until she was spent, until her breath was gone, until her throat was so tight and so dry it hurt.

She hammered through the sea wind some hundred metres or more, and then she slowed, suddenly emerging from a tunnel of fury, suddenly aware of the life in her muscles, the power in her chest, and the cold spits of sea salty water as they hit her cheeks. This was a harbour, and she had run a good part of its length without taking in any aspect, not a splinter of detail. Just running, wild and blind. But now that she stopped, she could see it. She could feel it, smell and taste it. Salt on the wind. The stench of seaweed bruising the air. Underfoot: mud and grassy patches, a tarmac road pitted with pot holes, gravel, stones. A sudden whiff of petrol, of kerosene, oil, and smoke. Dead fish. The tops of masts spiked her vision, followed by strange little stone buildings whose functions were hard to discern, too small for houses, too big for… she couldn't guess. Seagulls overhead, screamed and cawed up into the distance, flying far, swallowed into the bright white. She wiped her eyes, her cheeks felt fresh and warm; her feet, bare in sandals, cold. Sky, sky, sky…

She walked on quietly, getting closer to the harbour edge, watching her feet while walking, then picking up pace, creating rhythm, skipping along. Then stopping. A sudden shudder through her right leg, a sharp but short-lived spasm of pain in her knee. Leaning forwards she took in the sheer depth of the vast stone blocks underfoot, aware of their lack of response to her weight, though light, as her feet pressed down upon them. She carried on. The stones, absorbed her energy, gave nothing back. She took to planting her feet with all her might, as though a giant, making her claim on the wall and the land beyond.

Holding still once more, and looking straight out to a blue-grey distant sea, she held her position against the great tide of air as it whipped itself up off the water out there and so far away. Her hair danced upwards with the wind, swirling in an 'S' shape, feint lines upon the sky. Grass and warm summer tarmac were far more obliging when skipping, she pondered, acknowledging how the earth, deep beneath, allowed a little something of life to rebound. But the sea wall was different, a great fortress against the tide, it would not indulge mere skipping. It would not yield. This she fathomed. And this seemed right. She rubbed her knee and walked on slowly, breathing it all in.

The sea still some long way out, the boats hung down low and close inside the harbour wall. She peered down into the vessels moored up there. They leaned one into the other, partly settled in the mud below. Wood decks with curious doors here and there, some seemingly in the floor leading into the hull, the belly of the beasts; and then her gaze settled on the little house shapes, shed shapes, box shapes, some as though piled one on top of another, planted onto the decks. Some of these seemed to fit and Esther thought they looked quite right, others looked out of proportion somehow and awkward, too big or too small, or at an angle, set askew. The older boats a patchwork of woods, and subject to lesser and greater degrees of repair. Metal parts, knots in wood, paint peeling, the smell of fresh paint, the stench of rotting planks brought close on a sudden sheet of wind. Sails wrapped up tightly, loosely, shoddily; small flags whipped up by the sea air, or dancing gently when the flow of the wind softened and abated.

Further along she began to notice that there were people on some of the boats moored in a curved area of the harbour – the harbour 'proper' as she came to think of it. So far away, they looked tiny, like animated toys, each engaged in activity that played out in repeats. Pulling ropes, mopping decks, emptying buckets, and carrying buckets and boxes, and wood. And they were wearing T-shirts and wellies, and old shoes and fancy deck shoes; and some were in hats. Smart hats, as though for a captain, and ordinary hats, the type just to keep the sun off. Everyone was busy, there was chatter. Spikes of laughter. A shout. Some were giving instructions, people seemed to listen closely and then took up their tasks, checking back for detail or something misheard, lost to the wind. Esther wandered closer. 'Right you are!' was heard a few times, as people cheerfully took on some request, getting boats loaded up, or unloaded, fixing this or that. Esther walked on. There were more buildings further up. What looked like a great stone-built castle at the end of the harbour wall, later turned out to be the fisheries. And there was a great sand mountain, and a large metal vessel nearby, and a truck with the back at an angle suggesting it had just delivered sand from the ship. It must have taken a good many trips back and to, to unload all of that – Esther speculated how many. The sand pyramid, it was colossal. Esther would ask someone what that was all about. What was it doing there? What was all the sand for?

Everything felt so very different 'down the harbour'. She felt her heart rate coming back into rhythm with the rest of her body, she felt more real, more ordinary, more alive, not stiff, not mechanical. In the distance she could see the sea. It was coming in. No, it was still heading out. Or? She couldn't tell. She wanted to know.

There was an old seaman on an old fishing boat further on. He wore a nice navy blue hat, like a real true fisherman. She called out 'Excuse me,' a few times but the wind scattered the sound. 'I, I…' then she waited until she was closer and knelt down on the edge to be as near as she could be. The wind had dropped and when she yelled 'I was just wondering…' the fisherman half leapt in surprise.

'Jesus!' he tipped his hat at the front a little in order to see better, 'What d'you want there?'

Esther laughed. 'I was just wondering, sorry, about the sea…

'Never be sorry about the sea.'

'I meant…' she laughed, 'I have a question…'

'You watch your step there, you might slip and the wind's up!'

'Just a quest…' Her hair blew in front of her face; she wobbled.

'*Mind you don't fall… oh, Lordy…* best you come aboard.' He motioned to the ladder and held the base as he beckoned her down. 'Keep a hold,' he guided, 'one step at a time, there.'

Once aboard, he took a pipe from his pocket and propped it in his mouth. From a wicker basket on deck he produced a paper bag, 'Here, have an orange while I have my tobacco.' And this time he laughed. His laugh was chuckly and warm.

It was less windy down on the boat with the protection of the harbour wall. Esther thanked the old man for the orange, which she noticed was very round and very orange. She struggled to peel it, all the time her eyes set on the activity of tobacco taken from a pouch, observing how it was tugged at and gathered into just the right amount in the centre of the old man's palm before being settled into the bowl of the wooden pipe. Best of all was the lighting of the pipe. Esther, now totally distracted from her tide enquiries, watched as the man's cheeks grew fat with puffing, his white beard dancing like fairies at the edge of his face; and the flicker of light and then the smoke, and the aroma, not too unpleasant from a distance, just 'smoky'.

The old guy laughed again, 'Here, let me do that.' And with his hands finally freed up he took the orange from her and began to peel with skill. His nails were thick and hard like tools, his hands strong looking and woody. Esther regarded him.

'Peter, I'm Peter, young miss, but you can call me Pete.'

'Oh,' Esther thought for a moment, 'Well, I'm Esther, and you can call me... Esther,' she blushed at not being able to fathom an alternative.

'Nice to meet you, young Esther.' And he handed her a perfected peeled orange.

'Have a look about if you've a mind to, just watch your step... keep an eye on the ropes over there, plenty to trip on.'

'Alright,' Esher responded somewhat in awe and feeling quite privileged. She ate the orange segments as she stepped about with care, noticing the different types of ropes and the weave and knots in ropes, and ropes coiled up. She wondered how you tied them, and who had tied them, some looked rather heavy after all. She thought to ask, but Pete looked busy with something. She moved to the side of the boat and looked over the side, it stank and made her feel sick and light-headed.

'You alright there?' Pete noticed and called.

'Oh, yes, yes.' Esther didn't want to give the impression that being onboard was too much for her. 'Fine, Pete, thank you very much.'

He laughed and chugged away at his pipe.

Esther looked up and out at the sky, the birds were back, swooping but high up and far. A thick gust of wind would suddenly take her breath. She braced herself, shivered, and when the wind subsided permitted herself a moment of calm. She stretched out her arms to make like the birds, and swooped about the deck. She looked up and giggled imagining that the old fisherman might be watching, but his head was down, his hands busy with the nets. He kept the pipe in place all the while. His jaw steady. Esther looked back out to the sea and wished that it was closer, wished that it was higher and more blue, wished that she might stand before it and feel its life. It felt a little lonely with it so far away.

Suddenly anxious, but without knowing why, and aware of time, but not aware of how much of it had passed, she retraced her steps carefully back across the deck and volunteered, 'I'd better go now.'

'Alright, m'dear. You watch how you go.' The old man set down his work and moved to hold the ladder steady as she climbed.

'Thank you for the orange, Pete.'

'A pleasure, Esther. But you know, you shouldn't talk to strangers…'

At the top of the ladder, she hopped onto the harbour edge. She smiled and looked back down, 'Oh, don't worry, Pete, I don't.'

Light as a fairy she skipped back home.

# 8

Back at the house, Esther asked the man about the sand pyramid at the end of the harbour, and it seemed she had finally hit upon on something he was happy to talk about. The sand deliveries, brought in from abroad, were supplies for the local cement works, and load by load would be collected by trucks in the coming days. It was a slow process he commented, with each 'sand pyramid' – he laughed a little as he used Esther's description, 'replaced with another as soon as the final grains of the last were scooped up. That satisfy you?' he asked, Esther nodded, and she smiled at him.

'You mustn't go near it though, it's not stable, liable to slip down and smother you,' and he spread his fingers wide and motioned his hands over her head as though to reinforce this fear. Esther pulled back. She gave a small nervous laugh. She wasn't worried for a moment about the sand, but his hands were too near somehow.

Esther liked that the man had not actually told her off for roaming around the harbour. If she was honest with herself she had partly told him that she'd been there as a minor provocation, a test, as though to see how strict he might be, how far he might think he could act or make attempt to discipline her. Mum, on the other hand, entered at the end of their exchange and was very put out that Esther had 'wandered off'. She asked Esther if she had spoken to anyone, she said she hadn't. 'And you didn't go anywhere I wouldn't like you to?'

This seemed unspecific and simultaneously complicated, and so again Esther answered that she hadn't. She paused at the kitchen door, silently checking for possible further response and to gauge the general mood inside the house. The man mentioned to his wife that he had warned Esther about the sand deliveries, and this he did in a tone that suggested he had dealt with everything, which Esther appreciated, and he said that there were a couple of other very good families on the port, lawyer and stockbroker, banker types with very good children, 'bright', who Esther had probably befriended already, or would do soon enough, so Maud needn't worry.

It was nice to hear herself included in their conversation, and nice to hear the man's voice with a warmer tone cast in her direction. Mum sounded much less anxious, and so, for the first time, all parties appeared something close to being soothed.

As Esther ventured up the stairs she could still hear them discussing her and 'the port', her mum calmly voicing minor concerns, and the man seeming to side with Esther and deeming her to be of a sufficiently sensible disposition to handle small adventures. 'Adventures' yes, that's what they would be, her 'portside adventures' – she skipped inside. And as for bearing a 'sensible disposition', well of course! Esther was surprised he hadn't noticed this before. Still, some grown-ups are less astute than others, she reflected, and it was kind that he should mention it to Mum.

Over the next days, the three settled into something of a routine. In the mornings, the man ate his usual breakfast which he pronounced '*break*-fast', and this caused Esther to giggle, until he frowned her out of it. He ate a *break*-fast of *mues-e-li* at precisely seven-twenty, leaving the house on workdays at pre-*cisely* seven-fifty-five. And this he did, Esther noticed, without brushing his teeth. Dinosaur teeth. It was clear now why proper brushing was essential.

Mum decided mealtime seating arrangements, and though Esther hadn't wanted to appear rude, she really didn't like to witness the muesli mouth each morning, and so began to take care not to be seated opposite. Maud would grimace as Esther shuffled her chair around to the end of the table, but nothing was said. Maud would serve the man breakfast while Esther helped herself. It seemed funny. Mum was now the maid, just like those in old dramas she had seen on TV at Easter and Christmastime.

# 9

Towards the last days of the summer holidays Esther's portside adventures grew. Mum had started a new role at a local textile company, something important as she had to give them advice and 'steer things', which Esther liked the sound of, and the man did whatever he did. Esther speculated that perhaps he was a spy. It seemed odd that his work was never given a name, and after a while she had given up asking.

Down on the harbour, Esther's friendly spirit saw her hopping on and off all manner of vessel, a curious mix of resident moorings and the temporary, always someone coming in, someone heading out. Tugs and trawlers, and larger commercial vessels from time to time, yachts of all sizes, and there was perhaps even a surplus of old wooden vessels that had seen so many revisions in their use over the years it might take an expert to discern their age and original use, each marked by now with modifications and repairs to suit the eccentricities, pocket and skills, of their current owner.

There were several families moored up indefinitely who came from who knows where. Esther delighted in the romance of this. It seemed to be a feature that the stories they told varied heavily on the listener. The details would concern: from where they hailed, where they had travelled and previously been moored, what they were doing, how long they might be staying and, had they always been boat dwellers? Accents shifted on the breeze as did degrees of familiarity and politeness. But none of this affected Esther, she was somehow trusted and privy to the truth, or some semblance at least, but she was ever curious, though never asked, about the variations in performance when strangers made enquiries of her friends.

There were fancy sail boats with beautiful people like people in films, and there were more ordinary boats sailed and maintained by more ordinary looking people, but everyone was ordinary, underneath, Esther noted. She would shrug 'Just people, really,' and smile and skip at the thought.

Pete soon grew accustomed to Esther's daily visits, soon buying extra oranges lest his sea mate get scurvy. And tea, though he didn't drink 'the stuff' himself.

'Why don't you drink tea, Pete?' she asked him, 'Everyone drinks tea.'

'Always been a coffee drinker young miss, coffee in a morning... yup, coffee in a morning, whiskey late afternoon. That's the way of sailors,' he tapped the bowl of his pipe upside down, readying it for fresh tobacco, and stealing a smile to himself.

'The way of sailors?' Esther laughed cheekily, and mimicking his voice, 'Well, tea in a morning, and juice, late afternoon. That's the way of Esthers.'

Today Pete had promised to take her out to sea 'All things being equal... tide and time,' he teased; and so, this day, Esther's morning sky was strewn with stars, with the sun and the moon and asteroids! But she must try not to let her excitement spill out too much, she liked Pete to think he could rely on her, that she was a more than capable crew member, and above all else, that she was not silly. Going out to sea takes concentration, patience and a lot of intelligent moves. She kept all this in her heart.

Pete placed his pipe to one side for a moment while he made Esther's tea. She was familiar with every inch of the boat by now. She was always curious about the cabin and amused, especially by the galley, which she felt was a big doll house kitchen or a tree house kitchen. She liked how everything fitted in: the narrow beds, a cupboard snuggly positioned above or below. Others hidden away. 'Everything has been thought of, hasn't it, Pete? Just like a house! You even have a loo! But... you don't have a bath,' she paused and ruminated on this, and not wanting Uncle Pete to be embarrassed added, 'but then you can sort of swim and wash in the sea I suppose... or something.'

'You seem to be finding your sea legs.'

Esther looked down at her legs not quite understanding, then looked back up to find Pete returned to his tobacco ritual. The slowness involved and the care he took always stopped her in her stride. There was something truly calming about this practice, the slowness of it, the stillness and considered moves. She decided then and there that when she was old enough, she too would smoke a pipe. She knew exactly how to gather up the correct amount of tobacco in the cusp of the hand and how to gently persuade it into just the right shape, how to load it into the pipe, how to light it and how to do the puffing with your cheeks. Pipe smoking. When I'm big, she said to herself. I will do that too.

Pulling her into the present, Pete uttered, 'You'll be back

to school then?'

'I'll be what?' she said, indignantly.

'School. Term will be starting.'

'Well, not yet.'

'They start back early here. You could find it's a week or more ahead of where you moved from. It's funny round here.'

Esther didn't respond. Couldn't be right. She pursed her lips, went to ask – I mean, how did he know this? But then she shrugged.

Pete was busy now readying things, the next voyage always in mind. He'd lived on the harbour for years, semi-retired but never retired, and with a personal history that changed as often as the shipping forecast. Stories about his past floated round the harbour, but it was mostly speculation, and to Esther he was always, and had only ever been a sailor, a sailor and no other.

Esther finished her task of checking on certain ropes, that they seemed secure enough, to be doing the job they ought to be doing, and to report on 'anything untoward' – a job Pete invented for her. After that she helped him, using all her might, to heave a sail this way and that, for this was one to be mended.

'Can we head out now?' Esther blushed, a phrase she'd heard many times on the harbour, a phrase she'd never used, 'head out' – in respect of the sea. It seemed so grand, so grown-up, and yet, subtle and powerful; she repeated 'Shall we head out? The tide looks just fine... don't you think?'

'I 'eard you,' Pete's eyebrows emerged and danced a little beneath his cap, 'well, why not,' he added, 'only a short trip mind, but just so we get the feel of the water. We can rely on the engine to take us today. You check down below that we've enough supplies, oranges and biscuits…'

'And tobacco!'

Pete smiled, touched by this, and nodded. He could be heard muttering about slack water and getting back long before, and being mindful of the strength of the tide. Esther was awed by this, and impressed by his concern for safety. As she climbed back on deck she puffed out her chest like a pigeon and held her shoulders broad.

'Provisions, all present and correct?' he asked her. Esther giggled and nodded.

Once they'd negotiated their way from the safe arms of the harbour there was a natural rush of adrenaline, for suddenly the elements were free. The wind, no longer contained by high harbour walls buffeted the small vessel and whipped itself around their bodies, 'Hold tight there!' Pete called to his shipmate who had settled herself up ahead. She nodded and made herself safe on the deck, holding tight, measuring her balance, feeling, assessing, the strength and weight of the waters beneath and all around, and the wind as it held and released her with all its might. It was terrifying, and thrilling, and a rush through every part of her body. She was aware of her frame, her weight, skin and muscles, her sight and hearing, her lightness, her strength. She was the sea, she was the air.

Later she laid down to rest in a bunk in the cabin, not to sleep but rather just to test it out. She found some juice and ate some of the biscuits, after a while taking some up for the Captain. 'It was time,' Pete said, time they headed home. 'You'll be shattered, young miss,' but he knew she was proud, that despite being so little she liked to 'pull her weight'. He tipped his hat. Shook his head. Smiled.

Back at the harbour, finally acknowledging her exhaustion and the strength of the wild sea winds, 'they belt the air right out of you betimes,' Pete would say, Esther decided it was time to head back home. In truth, Pete's assertion about the local schools, had left her feeling puzzled and a little unhappy. But it wasn't Pete's fault. He was probably just wrong.

# 10

As she made her way across the gravel and then the tarmac road, she began to notice a new configuration on the islands of grass and trees on the harbour-side. There were dogs. People. People and dogs, dotted about on the green. Motionless, seemingly, then springing into movement, then coming to rest again like a dance. Lone dog walkers with dogs on leads. Lone walkers, dogs running free. Clusters of dog-walkers, chatting to one another, a stray lead dangling to their side. And more dogs, these as though making their escape. Running now, fast as they could. Esther began to run behind, trying to catch their rhythm, trying to match their speed. Her sandy hair blowing in the breeze, whipping her cheeks as the wind flipped its course. The dogs pounding the ground up ahead.

She could hear melodies on the rise and fall of the air about her and hummed along, she joined the notes up in her mind, tracing their patterns in the colours they presented: dashes of vibrant blue, peacock green, a splash of tangerine, dots of yellow, violet. There was a sweet lemon taste in her mouth, sweet like sherbet lemons, and suddenly the world was golden, then strawberry, then blue, and everything felt nice. Everything was real. Everything was true.

Near the garden gate, she stopped and looked back a moment to assess. There were some big posh houses to the right that she hadn't taken in before, with families getting in or out of cars. Two cars, two families, perhaps all friends. The children roughly the same age as herself, perhaps a little older. They might be the people that the man had spoken of. You couldn't see Pete's boat from here, or any of the others in the inner harbour. You could see the tops of masts nearby, and tell at least when the tide was in, and you could see the boats as thy bobbed about or swayed at times with their own great weight and the burden of the swell. You could see the other buildings, and the fisheries far off. You couldn't see the sand mountain from that position. But you could of course see the people and the dogs. A pale-yellow Labrador was suddenly at her side, it leaned on her affectionately. Oh! Unbalanced for a moment, Esther laughed, and then patted the silky dog, its tail wagging, its body pulsing with adrenaline. It wasn't on a lead. Was anybody looking for it, worried where it might be? Perhaps it belonged to that man chatting to that lady... and anyway, she had better go inside.

# 11

Pete was right all along. The next day was a school day. The information dealt on re-entry to the house. There was a new uniform laid out upon her bed they said, and the man had kindly paid for this. He gave a big smile and moved his head toward her. Esther stepped back and he laughed as he pulled upright again. How had they shopped for these things without her? Mum chivvied her upstairs to try it on, she'd opted for the same size as before as Esther clearly hadn't grown. Hadn't grown? She wondered whether to take issue with this, but the confirmation that yes, it was the start of school, mixed with the idea of the man shopping for her clothes, was already, altogether too much, far, far too much. Contemplating further intrusion and misjudgement was impossible to juggle right now.

She was pushed and hurried by her mother into the bedroom and it felt almost as though the woman was attached to her back, *'Come on, come on,'* she called, with an overexcited finger-prodding to the shoulder. Esther felt a true confusion of emotions. The cool blue of the room felt calming as she entered, and the green of the trees out through the window, and the paler blue of the sky beyond. But a further poke in the shoulder and a disarming 'Well, try them on,' from Maud, and Esther was returned to the state of insult.

'They'll fit,' Esther offered firmly under her breath, and before Maud could utter a response, she added loudly, 'just like you said, I haven't grown.' And she swerved her mother's hand, a hand that was meant to stop her leaving, and ducking just slightly, almost in a dance move, she pounded the stairs.

'*Where are you going?*' trailed after her.

'Forgot something,' she headed for the door, and once again the gate.

He was still there, the pale-yellow dog. Clearly, he was waiting for her. She looked about but rather absently, that she might easily miss the person waving far in the distance, should there be one. How could someone abandon such a beautiful dog? She patted his head and they slipped into the garden unseen.

She introduced him to the herb garden, such as it seemed, perhaps just weeds; and then to the flower beds where they danced alongside the bobbing flower heads. He barked excitedly, Esther froze and looked back at the house, but no one came to the window. They crawled under the trees near the low-rise shrubbery and made a kind of den, settling themselves a short while on the soil and fallen leaves. There were crawly things. She brushed them off her ankles. The dog sniffed about and sat and panted, perhaps he needed water. She tiptoed into the house and rooted around the cupboards for a shallow bowl, carefully filled one with cold water and then walked with teeny tiny steps, so as not to spill it, out again to the garden. As she stepped onto the path the man could be seen at the gate, he had his back to her. He was talking to another man who was attaching the pale-yellow dog to a lead. Well! She turned her back and went inside. But at least she had taken care of the dog for a while, and had not simply ignored it.

It was time to eat, Mum called out, and then the plan was early to bed as it was the start of term the following day. Mum had said this smiling. And the man then added, 'A new school, new friends…'

'Mum, will you read to me tonight? Will you… for a bit… a bit?' Esther felt her chest grow tight, and as she spoke her words seemed to take on a higher pitch, and a thin whistling sound as though the words didn't much belong to her. The man laughed. Maud shot him a look which allowed Esther to recover herself a moment, 'Please…' and then she felt a blush of embarrassment but it made no sense, it was her mum, her mum.

'Well, 'face and teeth' dear, and then I'll come and tuck you in.'

'And will you read?'

'We'll see dear, now off you pop.'

Esther left the room taking steps backwards so that she could monitor the man's reaction to their exchange. He seemed given to eyebrow raising and to sighing. So rude. And not very fair. And quite annoying. Esther took the steps upstairs slowly, annoyed that Mum had said 'Face and teeth,' as though she was a baby. And she didn't need tucking in, although that was nice, and it hadn't happened much since they'd moved. But she liked to read with Mum. She could read by herself, but it was so lovely to share, and to hear the words aloud, bouncing around and around, or making you stop and think, and chat, it was fun, and sometimes emotional, and often they would giggle and make sounds from the stories or make up the voices of the people and the things, *all* of the things! Fairies and elves and talking dolls or trains or bears or trees! Bears and trees, she settled in her mind, were two of her favourite book things, when she considered the 'younger' books they read. With other books, she liked to think about what people said and why, and wonder what might happen to them next. Um, she thought, now adding dogs to the list of favourite book things.

# 12

Esther read to herself for a while, then stared at the moon and stars through the window, feeling the gentle chill of night-time from around the window frames. Somehow this felt nice. And after toing and froing for a time to check for signs of Mum coming up to read or at least tuck her in, she settled down to sleep with her bear, making her nose and his wet from a few sneaky tears.

In the morning, the atmosphere was somewhat military. Muesli for him, toast for herself, Mum having eaten long before. Esther had put on the new uniform with all it's cold creases, and new cotton, hard to the touch. The man commenting that she shouldn't describe it as hard, as this was very inaccurate.

'But you're not wearing it,' Esther piped up.

'Esther!' rebuked her mother.

'But how can he know, he is not wearing it. I am.'

Mum shot her a further warning look, Esther rolled her eyes. Everything was so tricky living with the man, in the man's house. It seemed that being rude was now all blurred and sticky, when all you were doing was speaking the truth and speaking with facts. It really wasn't like that when it was just the two of them. Not like that ever.

'No time for nonsense,' the man threw in, gathering up his newspaper and moving to fetch his coat. 'Come on. Apparently, I'm taking you in the car' he directed.

Esther looked at Mum who gave her a hug and a kiss good bye, 'Yes, go on, you've got a driver this morning, lucky girl.' The man rolled his eyes at this while Esther and Mum exchanged cheeky smiles, each with a nervous teardrop too close to acknowledge. 'Oh,' Mum scurried down the path after them, 'Listen Esther, it's Hardaker now.'

Esther looked puzzled.

'Your name.'

'?'

'Your name, pet, it's not Rathbone, not Esther Rathbone...

'Not, Esther Rathbone?' she responded, her brow wrinkled.

'No, Hardaker, Esther Hardaker now.'

'*I don't understand... why?*'

'Now come along,' the man intervened, 'let's get the day started, I've got to get to work.'

Mum attempted a further hug, whispering again 'Hardaker, remember,' as the man took Esther's arm and tugged her through the gate and to the car.

The gate made its heavy slam. Esther gave his back a dark stare.

On the journey the man observed the other drivers, their lack of skill at driving, many hadn't passed their test, women were slow to overtake when there was clearly room, *typical*, he would utter, somehow clacking his teeth over the word. And, '*blondes,*' he would say, as though this was something not nice or bad or something else that Esther couldn't quite fathom. It was strange to spend time with someone you didn't really know like this. He was Dad now. Was this alright? Was this what 'dad' is? Is this, *this,* all that it is? Moany, grumpy, with a lot of bad feelings about what other people do?

The car came to an abrupt stop as the brake was sharply applied and Esther slid forward on her seat in the back. He didn't get out of the car, didn't look around to the back seat to face the little girl, but spoke to her as they exchanged a prolonged stare in the rear-view mirror, 'So, here you are,' and was he smiling? Was that a smile? 'Don't look so worried, Love, you hop out and the lollipop lady there will see you over the road,' he was leaning forward now and pointing to the right beyond the bonnet of the car, 'then it's just through there, take note, you'll see the school gates and all the children when you just go down that lane there, or you can walk around the edge of the road, then it's first left if you go that way. Got that?' adding, 'Damn nuisance having to drive round here.'

Esther swallowed. She felt hot, and shivery. The shoes felt tight, the uniform was itchy.

'I said, off you go then, door handle's just there remember. Just there! Left, left, down! That's it.' And before she could respond he revved the engine, 'Shut the door!' – she did, and with a limp hand she went to wave goodbye. He did not see, he was watching for traffic to his right and then pulled away and did not look back. Esther sniffed, and the lollipop lady in her fried-egg yellow and white uniform helped her cross the road. She directed Esther just as the man had done, but Esther stood awhile, breathing. Only breathing. Where was she, even? A familiar cry from the sky, she looked up. Seagulls. Her cheeks flushed with recognition. The sea. She was still not far from the sea then. Perhaps not far at all.

The lollipop lady chivvied her on her way, for the school bell would ring and she would be late for assembly on her first day! Esther dragged her feet, and then made is if walking at a pace, but somehow in her mind she felt held back, as though by the wind, as though the elements intended she take a different route. She looked back at the woman in her white and yellow coat and managed a half smile of thanks. She took enough steps to sense she might be out of sight, looked back to check, and then she stopped and breathed again. Ahead, children poured in through the school gates, and down a slope towards the brown school building. She came up after them with the timidity of a ghost, and squeezed her hands tight together to check that she was real. The wind grew again and in the distance the birds cried out and flew wide and high.

'*Oi, Sticks!*' A boy stood in front of her. 'That's right, you, *Sticks*'.

Esther's brow furrowed. Sticks?!

'Skinny sticks, don't they feed you where you come from?' He laughed and ran to catch up a group of boys, updating them on what had just happened; the group then turning their heads and joining in with his laughter.

Esther tried to breathe in a deep way, and took the last steps into the building more boldly, sensing the need now to put on a front. She found a peg for her coat, feeling the shove to the shoulders of the mass of children as they swarmed into the cloakroom, and the same again heading to assembly. She asked if she was in the right spot and a couple of girls became friendly and explained 'how it all worked'. Esther smiled at them and swallowed so as not to appear upset. And why should she be? She was at school, a new school, all brand new, and you were supposed to go to school, it's what you did, it's what children did, and it would all be alright. These girls were very nice, they were being kind and helpful, and that always helps. They were sweet. Probably there would be a break in the middle of the morning, just like in her old school, and they would have some juice or milk or something and maybe a snack. She pushed her focus to the thought of fresh sustenance while the children all around her shuffled their feet and whispered through assembly, elbowing one another and passing on secrets and sometimes sweets. She suddenly felt a hit of anxiety, and likewise longed for something sweet to taste to soothe away the fear, the fear of the unknown, the day that lacked a map, the space uncharted, the people yet to be encountered.

The little girls from earlier, Emma and Rebecca, were now joined by a third: Marion, and together they guided Esther to the classroom, and settled her at a desk that would be hers. So far so good. Esther had put the boys from earlier on in the playground quite out of mind. She focussed on the good, the nice girls, the expectation of morning break and refreshment; and then her line of sight settled through the window. The light, white, bright, the sky that held all the birds that flew above the sea. And then abruptly she was aware of a gaggle of boys at her desk, staring up at her having crouched down low, and aping her smile as she took in what she could see and

what she wanted to see through the dirty glass pane. '*Ahhhh...*
' one of them mocked, 'Is it all *bew-ti-ful* out there, Sticks?' He
stood up and kicked her shin, and laughed again, 'Didn't
break,' he grinned, 'not this time...' the other boys mocked
with laughter and parroted the nickname. Just then Ms Butler
entered. She shuffled in cautiously on heavy hips, carrying the
children's hefty homework books.

The boys withdrew the moment they were aware of the
teacher and took their places, each at his desk, with just one
sneaking out of the room, some subtle hand gesture to his
*compadres* as he returned to the class of his own further along.

Esther was relieved to see the teacher, she sucked back a
tear, and dabbed saliva on her tender shin. Why were the boys
being so mean? Emma and Rebecca were chatting and
seemed not to have noticed, but then Esther's eyes met
momentarily with Marion's whose gaze seemed to suggest
that she had witnessed the boys' derision and perhaps also the
kick, and she smiled back at Esther in just the wrong way. Had
she enjoyed her pain? Esther felt her heart beat a little faster.
She drew herself tall in her chair and tried casually to look
away, as though she had not noticed Marion at all.

'Right then,' Ms Butler called them to order, and Esther
took comfort from the obedient response of the class. Ms
Butler seemed to command their respect and would undoubt-
edly take no prisoners should troublemakers be discovered.
Good.

Ms Butler then issued a small speech, partly to remind them
of what was expected of them this term, the schedule of

events, and tests, and then she took the register, calling each child out by name, with the child responding 'Yes, Ms Butler.' Again, Esther took some comfort in the order that was seemingly being imposed, and she allowed herself to relax. 'Hardaker' was called, then again and again. The children scanned back and forth for the child that did not respond.

Esther's world, she felt, was beyond this room, it was out through those large school windows somewhere; and just now she was taken by the subtle changes in the whiteness of the sky, how it had become opaque, how a pocket of blue suddenly presented itself and then closed over again, quite as though it had never been there.

'Esther, Esther! *Esther* is that *you?*'

Esther's attention was pulled back into the classroom abruptly. Ms Butler's face was red, fat and red. Saliva at the edges of a prickly mouth. The room was silent but the tension felt high, and Esther felt it as screaming, as a loud assault. And the voice came again, sharp, and impatient 'I said, is that *you?*'

'I…'

'Are you, Esther Hardaker?'

'I…'

'Well are you?… For goodness sake!'

'I…' Esther glanced back at the window for comfort, for the view of a flight path, in the hopes of glimpsing seagulls, and the reassurance of their distant cry.

Ms Butler was at Esther's desk by now. She slapped a wooden ruler on the side of it.

'Esther,' the little girl answered softly. 'I'm Esther,' and she tried to smile.

'Esther Hardaker...?'

'Yes, yes...' though she didn't feel sure. What had happened? Something had happened. Everything was strange, everything was odd, and new, and the sort of new that isn't really good or nice. Everything had moved. Everything was in the wrong place and had the wrong feeling. Her head felt light. She tried to place her feet solidly on the floor, to feel the hardness, the stillness, the real. But somehow, seated at chair height, she couldn't quite reach, she couldn't feel. She gripped the sides of the desk, lest the world spin out of control.

'It seems our new friend, isn't sure of her name...' and with that the classroom erupted into shivering laughter. They parroted their teacher 'Yeah, doesn't know her name'. Marion looked at Esther now with a clear smile that was the opposite of smiling. Esther's chest felt tight. She had to do something, somehow stand her ground, demand their respect.

'I know my name, I know my name. It's Esther, Esther Hardacre. E, S, T, H, E, R...' she gulped a breath down and stood up, feeling the return of her confidence.

Ms Butler seemed to be granting her this moment to gather herself and save face, and, looking over the brim of her glass, offered an encouraging 'Yes...' and ushering her to continue.

'H, A, R, D, A, C, R, E!' The final 'E' felt satisfying and Esther permitted herself the briefest smile.

'Not what I've got down here, m'dear...' Ms Butler, now back at her desk, perused the register. The class began to titter again. Ms Butler shushed them.

'No, rather, it is: H, A, R, D, A, K, E, R!' And with that nothing could hold back the class who met this with vicious rapture. Esther slumped back down in her chair. She angled her head towards the desk and closed her eyes, and she held herself like this for several moments. She wasn't there, she wasn't there, all of this was dreaming… and it couldn't hurt, it really couldn't hurt, because it wasn't true, wasn't real, none of it.

'Did I say you could sit?'

What? Had Ms Butler said this? Esther had stood up of her own volition, why should the woman now take issue with her sitting down?

Ms Butler continued, 'I said, did I…?'

'You didn't. I don't think…' Esther looked up towards her, 'but I would like to sit down now.'

One of the boys took on her voice, or so he thought 'Ooh… but I would like to sit down now.'

Ms Butler curtly reprimanded him, and then told Esther that best she try and work on her spelling as she was far too old not to be able to spell her own name fully. Giggles shot round the room. These were followed by Ms Butler's heavy gaze and this time were cut short. Esther felt tears pushing through, though she tried her best to hold them back.

Ms Butler spoke again, 'Oh, dear me. Well, not to worry, if you are behind with other things as well, we can see about putting you in a special class or perhaps you could even be moved down a year.'

Esther took a tissue from her pocket and stemmed the flow

of distress. She looked directly at Ms Butler and stood again, 'I have no problem spelling, or anything else. I don't need special classes and you won't put me down.' Then she sat back down in her chair again, heavily, and crossed her arms. She closed her eyes once more to maintain composure.

Somehow it was as though the matter had ended and Esther managed to make it through day one. It had not been a nice day, it had not been a good nor an interesting day except for meeting Rebecca and Emma, but it was done. School was out and she could head back home.

As she walked up the slope to the school gates she scanned the clusters of parents. Mum wasn't there, she must be working. Of course. But what if Mum had instructed the man to pick her up? She hoped not. She stopped scanning, put her head down at an angle and marched out of the playground, seeing nothing, hearing nothing. At the corner of the road she breathed. Opposite the school corner was a post office, a very tiny post office. She crossed over and peering through its smudgy windows made out a very tall man with a beard, a very fluffy-at-the-edges, very thick and hedge-like beard. Round glasses, and brown… yes, most likely brown eyes behind them. She could not read any expression due to the amount of foliage taking over his face. There were the usual post office things, a counter, leaflets, but it was hard to make out more. A hand took her shoulder, 'There you are!' It was a warm voice. It was Mum. Yes! And she had come to collect her on her very first day at school. Esther beamed. They took a moment to hug. 'I thought, I'd fetch you on your first day, and if we walk back in the sunshine then you'll know the way and be able to do it on your own.'

Esther took a moment to take this in, registering that being picked up today by Mum was an exception. But that she had come today was a glorious thing and suddenly there were trumpets playing, fading gently into mandolins. And the world was warm and yellow, then apple green.

Since they were at the post office, Mum thought to pick up some stamps, and perhaps Esther would like some sweets. Would they have sweets? They entered, and the smudginess lifted. They did have sweets. Lots. In old fashioned jars behind the counter, sold by weight; in packets of all sizes; and best of... best of all... in open boxes, all different kinds, that you chose as you liked and paid per sweet. Liquorice sticks, some of the hard kind that grown-ups prefer, some filled with coloured sugar; and then small sweets in wrappers; cola bottles, shrimps and flying saucers... Esther breathed in their sugary fragrance while Mum got her stamp order. And when Mum turned around and nodded consent, Esther chose a good few and took them to the counter. The man in the foliage seemed to smile, it was hard to tell, but he had a warm atmosphere and Esther decided then, that beards might be rather good markers for nicer men. Pete had a beard.

Esther noted the route back home, but at the same time she was aware that there was more than one, for there was certainly a way to head to the harbour that missed out the main part of the town, and didn't involve passing the house if you were heading to the inner harbour. This could be done if you cut through a small park that divided the road from the harbour. Esther remarked that there was perhaps more than one route, and Mum agreed, but they settled that the one they were taking was the most direct and perhaps best in terms of least busy roads for when she took the route on her own.

'Do I have to go to that school?' Esther enquired, 'Is there any other?'

'Didn't you like it? It's just the first day, dear. First days are always tricky, but I'm sure you'll settle in, and you always make friends.'

'I did make friends... Emma and Rebecca. But...'

Mum was now preoccupied with watching for traffic left and right and reminding Esther how to do the same. Esther rolled her eyes. It was just a road and she wasn't five.

'Oh, you made some friends already, and on your first day! Well done, well done.'

Esther allowed herself to be lifted by the compliment; she might try to explain more about her day at bedtime. Probably Mum would come and have a proper chat then.

# 13

That evening there was some sort of disagreement between Maud and the man and Esther was ushered up to bed rather early. 'Face and teeth, dear.'

Esther hovered. There was a moody silence from the adults, then Mum said again, 'Face and teeth…'

'But…I need to tell you something…'

'Your mother said, bed.' The man had a stern look.

Esther wanted to correct him, but didn't. Either way, she was in the way, and was sent away. Closing her eyes and walking backwards through the hallway, melodies began to form, she could hear the instruments coming into play as though she had bidden them to do so, and she chuckled, for actually they came all by themselves. She bumped into the walls a few times, but since she moved with tiny steps it didn't much hurt.

The violins were serene, and then the viola… was it? Her arms moved forwards as though to conduct. Streams of pink and lilac coiled like ribbons, yellow, then mandarin orange. She sensed the taste of sugared almonds. Then raspberries. She paused and took a breath. She opened her eyes and found the cool shadows of the entrance. She danced there awhile. At the bottom of the stairs she remembered Africa and it made her smile. It was some time since she had seen her friends there.

She pushed the heavy door. It was especially cool with pale orange light at the window. She smiled at the masks awhile, chattering to them in her mind about her day. She ran her hand over the ebony elephants, tickled the chins of the giraffes and laughed. She laid down next to Zebra. Zebra. Poor Zebra, she thought and closed her eyes.

She woke to shouts, and sat up sharply. He stood over her, a gargoyle in the shadows, everything about him fixed in rage, 'I have told you, have I not told you…?' Mum stood behind now in the doorway, without words and that 'oh, dear me,' look. Esther reached out to her in heart, in mind, casting a desperate look asking for help.

But 'Oh, dear me,' was all that she offered, and then she retreated.

Esther wanted to stand, but his position leaning inwards and over her seemed to prevent it. She shifted around on her bottom and leapt up to one side, but not wanting to appear to be running away, stood with strength and gained her balance. She wouldn't cry. Never. He yelled and yelled. He had told her before, and she had no right, what was she doing in his room, touching his things…

'But they are just things,' she smiled and shrugged, 'I don't mean any harm.'

For a moment, he was speechless. It was hard to know what this meant and hard to know what was to come.

He let his arms fall to his sides, dropped his head, turned and muttered indecipherably and left the room.

Esther permitted herself a huge sigh and looked about the room. It seemed so silly. She glanced her little hand over the backs of the elephant family, and quietly went up to bed. Was she wrong? Really? *Really*, was it bad to go to Africa? How could it be just his? How could the animals be his? Zebra had a body once, innards, and… and legs! And its own life. Its very own life. Never was it his. Esther sat and watched the darkened sky from her bedroom window, and the stars there shining bright. And she settled her thoughts on the matter, no, no and no, one man did not own Africa, and he didn't own those bloody animals. She blushed at the swear word even though it only ran through her mind. Bloody idiot, she thought, looking round lest anyone be around and somehow read the thought.

She climbed into bed. And just before she fell asleep, it occurred to her, that despite his being wrong and mean, the man seemed somehow upset, and also rather unhappy with her. And though she knew not why entirely, she took it upon herself to try and win him over, to make a friend of him. They were a family now after all. Like other people's families. She remembered that she had planned to draw or paint for him, or perhaps write him a poem. And perhaps all three!

# 14

When she woke, there were several small watercolours on her desk, a jar of coloured water, brushes and the watercolour set all laid out. She yelped with glee. She didn't remember doing this, but it happened sometimes, that when the rhythms took her, and even in her sleep, she would half wake and paint or draw, compose a small piece of music, or move words around until they found some form.

She was delighted by the find, the sun shone in, she bid a very good morning to the tree outside her window, to the grass, to the clouds, sky and sun. And choosing that which she deemed to be the very best of the pictures, she hurried down-stairs to *break*-fast... giggling.

Since the painting held all the colours of Africa, that became its title. It was bright and warm, she could feel the local heat, she could hear drums, laughter and dancing. People were busy with all aspects of life, and the animals wandered freely in the distance where the sun grew hazy.

She entered with the painting and proudly presented it in front of her, beaming with smiles that came like a generous tide, over and over. Mum looked around 'What are you gig-gling at, little miss?'

The man was museli-ing and looked up from his bowl.

Mum tapped the man on the shoulder from behind in case he hadn't seen, 'Look, look! I think it might be for you,' and then addressing Esther, 'it's wonderful! And what are you calling it?'

'Africa! Because it's Africa…' she looked down at her work to check she'd picked up the right one, and it was.

The man made a noise, a sound, a mouthing of something not discernible.

Mum asked him to respond. This took some time.

'I said, it's nothing like Africa.'

'Oh, it is, it is dear… Esther always does quite abstract pieces…'

'Does she now…' he got up from the table and turned heading to the sink to drop his bowl there, 'nothing about Africa, she knows nothing about it, never been.' E s t h e r stood, indignant. It was true, she had never been, but she had seen documentaries and photographs, she had a 'sense' of it, a feeling. And wasn't the painting nice?

Mum smiled in consolation, hinting in her glance that she would smooth things over.

'Ten years. I was ten years in *Keen-ya..*'

'Kenya, wasn't it darling?'

'Don't correct me. Ten years I was in Keen-ya with my family. Very different world. Very different.'

Esther held Africa in just the one hand now, by the corner. Bemused. She was slightly transfixed by this unexpected reaction, and listened to try and glean why it was wrong to have painted Africa when you haven't been there.

'Children,' he shot her a look, 'seen and not heard. Manners, true, true manners, something I have held good to since I was a boy. There was order. Decent houseboy, housekeeper, not much more you need really. And people knew things then, they knew their place.'

Esther's brow crinkled up, what did he mean? What's a houseboy? How did people know their place? What was that? And he still wasn't explaining why you shouldn't paint a place when you haven't been there. She wanted to tell him that she often painted the planets...

Mum suggested she take her 'nice picture' upstairs, perhaps they'd put it up on her wall later with some others, and start an exhibition. But for now, she had better go and get her coat and school bag, whilst she quickly made toast – the man had kindly offered to take Esther to school again.

She barely ate, then she followed the man out to his car, kicking at the tiny stones on the surface of the road.

The day undone, Esther let a trickle of tears descend to her short collar without capture. Her tissue firmly in her pocket. The man talked at the road, at the windscreen, and to *God Almighty* quite a lot. There were still too many learner drivers on the road, too many women, too many blondes pulling out and overtaking without *'bloody looking!'*

As he pulled into the curb near to the school, he told her again what a damn nuisance it was to have to drive out of his way before his day started.

She pushed the door outwards and puked into the gutter. 'Dear god...' the man tutted. Esther wiped her mouth with her tissue and embarrassed, let her sandy hair shroud her face.

'Well shut the ruddy door!' He drove off.

The lollipop lady came to her rescue and patted her gently

on the back, asking if she was alright. Esther nodded and sloped away toward the school. As she reached the other side of the road she spotted several small coins on the pavement edge. She picked them up and brushed the bits of dirt off them and put them in her pocket. She eyed the post office as she passed by, 'later', she thought, later she would have sweets.

# 15

After what seemed to Ms Butler, a very long morning, she asked the children to each write a story. They were given free rein over the subject matter, Ms Butler having grown exhausted by the demands of her role and a new child that she was finding increasingly difficult, which mostly had to do with 'mathematics'. It had been brought to Ms Butler's attention that the new child, along with two other friends at said child's previous school, had always been set far more complex mathematics questions than their peers, and the teacher there had been very happy about this, very happy indeed.

'Well, that was then, and this is here and this is now, and you will do what everyone else is doing. There's no special treatment here.' Ms Butler refused to be challenged.

The class had been set a series of simple mathematics equations to work through, however, at this school you had to call it 'maths' and not show off. Not quite understanding this, Esther attempted to assert that the word *is* mathematics.

'Well so it might be, somewhere else,' Ms Butler growled, 'but here it's *maths.*'

This encounter quite perturbed Ms Butler, for whom even basic 'maths' was quite a struggle. Esther bolted through the tiny puzzles on the board, and in no time at all had correctly completed a lesson's worth in just seven minutes. The bickering that followed consisted largely of an exchange of multiple versions of, '*well, you can't have done,*' met with, '*well I have*', and, *'well they won't be right'* and *'I think they will be.'*

Four times, Ms Butler was caused to add more 'maths' to the board, and four times Esther completely all without mistake, five including the first batch.

It was hard to understand that being good at mathematics could be construed as showing off, but so it was, and what Esther didn't realise was that *that sort of behaviour* is punishable, and that it would indeed *be* punished.

Esther was not pleased that the equations were so easy, she wondered if should write some of her own next time, that would be exciting, and all Ms Butler would have to do is check if they were right. Perfect.

For story class, Esther decided to write about the moon. She wrote the title and date at the top of the page as prescribed and let her thoughts run. Though the morning had been less than pleasing on her side too, at least she had a nice plan for what to do next time they had mathematics, and story writing was always a huge pleasure, especially when you could write whatever you liked. This last thought raised her opinion of Ms Butler, who didn't seem naturally inclined to free thinking.

At the end of the class, each of the children had to hand in their rough book at Ms Butler's desk. Esther had added drawings to her moon story, and when Ms Butler flicked through her book, as she did with every third or so child, she scoffed at the images, for art remained in the art class. The children standing close by giggled. Marion, who wasn't far away either, looked on with an air of superiority. What a day it had been.

Truly, what a day. But then Esther remembered the coins in her pocket, the promise of sweets; and she also decided that when she got back to the harbour she would look for any dogs out on their walks.

At home-time she noticed Emma and Rebecca and tried to chat as they set off home, but the two, though still smiley and friendly, seemed to have a special friendship, their mums knew one another, that sort of thing, and they met them at the gates—and Esther was already aware that 'three' was a tricky number. But at least they seemed somewhat friendly and sometimes asked a nice question. She skipped away, encouraged by the thought of post office sweets.

High on sugar, Esther made it back close to home. She paused at the gate. It seemed just too early for 'them'… for Mum and the man, ohhh, too early to talk to 'them', and not talk to 'them', and though most likely they wouldn't be back until later and she wouldn't have to experience of any of this just now, she didn't want to be in the house either, with its echoes of them. She popped in just long enough to abandon her school uniform and pull on her favourite tree-climbing jeans, t-shirt and trainers. Mum said the jeans were ready for the bin, but they had special pockets and she favoured that particular denim blue.

All prepared, she headed for the green near the houses with the neighbouring children of lawyers and bankers. Their cars pulled up, their mums having collected them from their own schools. Esther stood proudly, suddenly in possession of a cheerful idea. New friends, neighbourhood friends, she would wait for them to get out of the cars and introduce herself, quite in the way she had seen grown-ups do.

The children in the nearest car looked on and waved. This was all very promising. When they were out of the cars and had collected up various school bags, Esther moved towards the vehicle and announced 'Hello!'

A girl and boy giggled and smiled 'Halllooooo!' in return.

The mum said something to them that Esther couldn't quite catch, except for '...one of the boat children.' And she ushered her offspring into the house.

Boat children?

The girl and boy looked back at Esther nonetheless and waved a mixed hello and goodbye sort of wave. The children in the second car, the more distant car, had already skipped into their house further along, so no chance for an introduction there.

Esther wandered near the inner harbour to look for Pete. When she found him he said he was very busy and she'd best come back another day.

'But, but what are 'boat children'? Can I just ask that?

'Oh, probably the landlubbers referring to the families along here,' he motioned to an unspecific spot further along the harbour, 'the families that live on their boats there. Mostly their parents lost jobs, lost their homes, you know... run into difficulties over money, that sort of thing. Or sometimes there's a family that have chosen boat life, but that seems the rarer case.'

'Oh...' and not quite understanding, 'and am I one, am I

'boat children'?'

'Are you heck as like. Not that it'd matter, but no…' he looked up at her for the first time since the start of their exchange, and he beamed at her 'not a jot, you're a sailor, just like me.'

Esther laughed and threw her head back and took in the sky. 'I'll come back another day…' she said, half stating the fact, half asking.

'You'd better!' Pete called warmly as she skipped away.

She swung her arms and began to sing 'You're a sailor, proper sailor, just like me.'

On the green running headlong were two pretty dogs, Spaniels. They were off their leads and racing for their lives, hurtling towards an invisible finishing line. Esther overtook, her throat was dry, the air burned her chest as she ran full pelt. She stopped and bent double to catch her breath. The dogs jumped up and said hello. The dogwalker was nowhere to be seen. She opened the gate and without hesitation, in they ran.

At around six in the evening, a weary and worried dog-owner found herself at the Hardaker gate. The harbour master had suggested that the tall walled garden might be of interest to the lady's dogs, and that a small blonde child might also have a particular fondness for four-legged friends.

Mum wasn't pleased about the dog story, what was Esther thinking? How many times had she done this now? Why did she keep doing it? It was alright to think you are just taking care of someone's dogs, but actually those people were missing their dogs.

To Esther's surprise the man piped up that perhaps they should consider getting her a dog, her own dog. *What a stupendously brilliant idea!* Her heart leapt. The man had owned dogs before, and they needn't be a lot of bother. And if they got her a dog then she wouldn't have to take other people's. Except that Maud really couldn't bear animals. It wasn't that she didn't care about them, and she never liked to think of them coming to any harm, but she didn't like their warm bodies, and it seemed inevitable that at some point you did have to come into physical contact with them, even by accident, putting out food for them, or when they jump up at you. And what about all the hair? On the furniture, everywhere, it would get everywhere. Absolutely everywhere.

It was an odd moment, a truly bizarre moment in fact, in which for once, Esther and the man's thoughts converged. What a strange woman Mum could be. Had the man and Esther been on a better footing they might have exchanged a knowing glance. But it was enough that the suggestion of this was in the air.

Mum quickly changed topic, and wanted to let Esther know that at the weekend they would be having a small gathering at home, a sort of mini late summer party for a few grown-up friends. Maud couldn't settle on whether to call it a 'late summer' 'party' or a 'hello autumn' 'do'. 'Hello autumn!' said the man, 'ridiculous, Woman.'

'Well…' Maud was piqued, 'then, 'late summer party' it is,' she wiped down the kitchen side again.

Esther had quietly been taking this in, so, grandparents

coming? No. Would Paul and Anne be coming? Unfortunately not, they were on holiday in Venice or somewhere, Italy anyway – but there would be plenty of other nice people and perhaps some of the neighbours, and perhaps their children, though they were hoping for a child-free event, just for once. Esther was to be counted in amongst the grown-ups, a sort of promotion so to speak, and she pulled herself up tall. Mum suggested she could wear her bridesmaid dress. Esther looked perplexed, and uttered a very weak 'Well… actually…'

Mum looked at her forcefully and didn't blink, 'Well wouldn't you like that? It would be fun to dress up? No?'

'It's just…' Esther wasn't really sure what she meant or what she wanted to say. In short, it just felt odd. The man interjected, 'Best make the most of opportunities to wear that dress, all that money. Or you'll have grown out of it in no time.'

Esther wanted to correct him in this, since it seemed unlikely that would happen 'ever' as she didn't seem to grow anymore. This was all too confusing, dogs, dresses, people, parties, weren't they talking about getting her a dog? Well, weren't they? Now it was all about some dratted dress. And an idiots' party. She turned and headed to Africa. Mum and the man were now completely immersed party plans, who to invite, indoors or out? But at least this meant the coast was clear.

By now she knew why she didn't want to wear the dress, it was a stupid dress. Oh, and why were Anne and Paul in Venice? She tried to picture Venice, but the image lacked detail and came out just as the reflections in puddles do, somehow pretty but entirely unsharp. The man was still talking loudly in the background, Esther felt this interfered with her brain-waves, and the beautiful could only fail to make its way through. And surely Venice would be beautiful? But at least there were violins playing now, and softly. Was that Venice? Probably, yes, probably it was, it didn't seem as though it would be Africa.

The day, yes, it had been too much. Would they, would they buy her a dog? She closed the door and settled herself in the centre of Africa and took counsel from her friends.

# 16

At school next day Ms Butler announced that classes would be conducted in the language of their forefathers. She would begin by taking the school register, and trusted everyone had learned at home what she expected them to know. Some of the children giggled but this was soon crushed by a glance over the brim of her glasses. Rebecca and Emma smiled at Esther, but they also looked concerned and mouthed 'You'll be OK.'

Esther smiled back at them but didn't understand. Marion shot Esther a mean look, but by now Esther had grown accustomed to these. It might even seem strange if Marion was ever nice.

Esther hadn't ever considered what a local dialect could be, but she liked to learn new things so perhaps the day would simply be more challenging.

Ms Butler conducted the register in her native tongue, but since the names called out were entirely recognisable, Esther was so far completely undisturbed by the shift in language. And when it came to her turn, approximately half way through the register, she had heard the response offered by the other children a sufficient number of times so as to mimic the sound rather well. She blushed when she spoke, and some children giggled, but Emma gave her the thumbs up and others were also smiling, and all was well. Her first attempt at a word in a language new to her. She felt warm inside. But when she looked up, Ms Butler's face was red, the red of fury. But why? Ms Butler broke into English, 'Oh, I see, so you think you're clever now do you?'

Esther didn't respond.

'Well, Ms Clever Clogs, why don't you introduce yourself to the class now, tell them where you come from, what your mum and dad do, what your hobbies are, what you think of your new school here, eh?'

'Well…' Esther stumbled.

'Go on then.'

'Well, I come from…'

'Not in English, not in English Ms Clever Clogs. We all know English, but we all know our own language too. So, if you're going to be part of things, then let's hear you.'

Some of the boys parroted, 'Yeah, let's hear you!'

'I….' Esther stuttered, everyone was staring, waiting, waiting like the meanest, rottenest things. Waiting, waiting, waiting. Ms Butler didn't scold the boys, in fact she seemed to delight in their bating. The children sat more upright, taking position, staring in hostile union, with the only the exceptions: Emma and Rebecca who slumped back in their seats and seemed desperately to be trying to communicate something kind through the ether. A hug at least.

Suddenly, Ms Butler slapped her wooden ruler across Esther's desk, as though marking the start of battle. And then, as though responding to orders, the children starting to goad Esther, 'Come on Ms Clever Clogs, *speak, speak!*' until the room was filled with an incessant chant and stamps of feet.

Ms Butler called a halt to this, as though suddenly realising the nature of what she had started, as though she was aware of the hate generating, as though knowing this was wrong. But then she ordered Esther to stand on her chair. And perfectly bewildered, Esther obeyed. She stood on her wooden chair, and one of the girls pointed to her thin legs and screamed out 'Sticks, sticks!' The room erupted in laughter. Ms Butler joined them, and together they pointed and chanted 'Sticks, sticks!' A thunderous eruption of chants.

Ms Butler called her army to quiet themselves again. She moved close in on Esther, holding the wooden ruler in her left hand all the while. Marking the child's position on the chair.

'So… speak girl, speak!'

Esther remained silent, her cheeks flushed, her heart pounding with fear, her mind travelling at high speed desperate to fathom what on earth she should do. What do you do? Held up for ridicule, danger all around, only the clouds and the trees beyond the school windows for comfort, and all too far away. You simply cannot think fast enough and cannot reach an answer. Her brow furrowed and she remained entirely silent. And still. Her own thoughts distracted her, she seemed composed and Ms Butler wasn't pleased. Ms Butler looked around the room at her audience, her army, and reassured that she had their full attention and assuming the loyalty of each, she turned her attention again to Esther, 'So, not a word. You cannot speak one word of our language, and yet you come here, you come here to live, and you come to 'our' school…'

the class echoed 'our school', 'yes, 'our' school and you try to tell us how you did things differently, *better* at your old school, because you're smarter than the rest of us, aren't you, *Sticks?* And yet, you can't speak a word.'

Esther couldn't hold back anymore, and the tears that had risen from so deep inside fell with the full weight of her pain. She couldn't speak. She still barely had the concept of another language, she had no energy to gather thoughts, or form words, any words at all.

Ms Butler was unfazed, 'If I had a parrot in a cage it could speak more than you can.' The class melted once more into laughter and Esther was made to stand on her chair for the remainder of class whilst Ms Butler continued her lesson, pausing only for occasional mockery.

After school, without coins for sweets, Esther ran like the wind to get home. No one there. She fetched a blanket from the house and lined her den under the trees with it, quite out of sight, and made it more of a home. A place that was hers.

She ran back inside the house desperate for refreshment. There was orange juice in the fridge and that was sweet and delicious, and there were biscuits in the tin. She took a few in her hand and went to sit outside the gate and watch the world awhile. — A Dalmatian, funny and spotty, with tall thin legs. A few small dogs on super long leads that tootled about and looked like toys. And then an Alsatian. What a *beautiful, beautiful* dog. He too was on lead. She stared after him, willing him to look back, then willing the owner to set him free. She tapped her feet over the gravel and made up a tune in her head and tried to match it with the speed of the clouds as they waltzed overhead. She hummed, and so distracted, the Alsatian almost knocked her over with his introductory leap. Esther regained her seat and laughed. She looked down the harbour. Owner, nowhere in sight.

She named him Hero, and then took him into the garden where the two snuggled down in the den. He was absolutely the best dog to cuddle, no competition at all. She felt his warmth and let her heart settle into rhythm with his. Perhaps he could stay. That would be good! Perhaps he would stay forever.

# 17

The man came home, and close on his heels, Mum. What a day it had been. Esther acted swiftly and managed to return Hero to his owner, who strangely called him Basil, but though neither the man nor Mum were directly involved this time, things had not gone unseen, nor unreported.

In the kitchen, Esther refused to be questioned over the dog. She held her ground in silence while the adults thundered overhead. Esther clenched her fists and closed her eyes determined not to cry, and so much more than that, determined, when there was a moment of ease, a space just large enough, to speak about her day.

Exasperated, the two adults separated momentarily, one to put on the kettle, the other to open wine. The one opting for tea, without much persuasion quickly switching to the comfort of alcohol. Truly, what a day! Two glasses lifted from the draining board. With the adults now slightly sedated, Esther breathed and opened her eyes, she let her hands unfurl, and building from impassioned quiet, from intense composure, there followed a dramatic recounting of the school day and Ms Butler's behaviour. The man soon took to the living room with his newspaper, shaking it out as he went as though to shake away the women in his life, things he shouldn't have to deal with and weren't his concern.

By the end of the retelling, Esther was almost sodden with tears. 'My teacher might keep me down a year...' Maud wasn't going to let that happen!

'They don't even know me Mum, I haven't been given a chance!'

Maud decided that she would mention all of this discretely to her husband later, see if he had any thoughts, and one way or another she would sort it all out. But she failed to convey any part of this to Esther. She simply held her hand to her chin in contemplation. And so, it hung in the air, a little girl's fear, that she might be put down a year, that she was being so unfairly treated and that it would all just carry on, perhaps even, forever. *And they had no idea that she could do things, and that she could some things very well!* She wanted Mum to tell them that. But by now Maud felt her head spinning, it really had been one of those days, oh my, had it been; and though giving herself credit for being on top of this, she somehow managed to prioritise in quite the wrong order. She would look at everything, 'deal' with everything, but just now she needed this wine, and a minute just to herself, and please, oh please, would Esther stop taking blankets from inside the house and using them to line woodland!

Esther, now entirely spent, collected up the blanket from outdoors and lay it, leaves, soily twigs and all, roughly over her bed. It had Hero's scent and fur on it. She snuggled down into it and slept.

Downstairs, further discussion was pursued over what became known quite firmly as the 'dog issue', and now that Maud had fully digested what had happened at school that day, she finally relented. Perhaps it *would* be best if Esther had a pet of her own. Might lift her spirit, give her some sense of responsibility. As long as it was known, that the conditions of a dog becoming part of their lives were explicit and must be adhered to: it would have to be a dog that was already house-trained, and Esther would have to take responsibility for feeding it, walking it… and on a proper lead; and clearing up its room… well, it would have to sleep in the small room adjacent to the pantry, or the deal was off, it simply could not sleep in the house itself, as Maud would not, NOT, tolerate dog hair.

And so, since the man didn't much mind having dogs around, it was agreed that they would ask about and try for a rescue dog or some such. Besides, he wanted something done about Esther's dognapping. It was bad enough that it was very close to full-on thieving, but more than that he didn't want gossip spreading about what a strange child she clearly was. Maud was affronted by this, but also embarrassed, and she chose to let it pass.

# 18

In the morning Esther felt a pounding in her heart. She sat up in bed in her pale blue room and looked toward the window and the tree. She breathed, and she could hear that breath. She held the edges of the sheet and looked about for Teddy. He was there, on her pillow. She cuddled him. But bad thoughts were pushing themselves to the front: *school, Ms Butler, the smell of the cloakroom, the tuneless piano at assembly, the boys who sometimes pinched her arm, the tittering and shoving and sometimes a kick.* Was it possible, I mean, was it really, truly possible, that it was morning again already? And was it possible another day had been created without her having had time to prepare?

It turned out that Mum had left early for a breakfast meeting. Great. Esther sighed heavily. Mum's absence made it easy to skip breakfast. The man was busy with his muesli and didn't seem to notice what she did. There was no way she could eat. She wandered about the kitchen and stood awhile behind him. There were just minutes before they'd have to leave. The sun shot across the counter near to the sink and the draining board. She noticed a handful of small change on the kitchen side to the right of the drainer. It was the man's money. She was about to tell him, remind him 'Don't forget your change!' when she stopped herself. A few of the coins were separated off from the main pile as though they were not really all the same money, not really all the man's money, or might not be, and yet she knew it was. It was wrong to steal. But it was just small money. Was that different? People on the news went to prison for stealing. She might go to prison. But that was a big bank robbery, like in a film. And they had stolen millions! Simply millions! Would you go to prison if you just took three of four small coins?

The man got up and belched. He left the room without looking back and then called from the hallway to 'Get a move on'.

Perfect. If she wasn't meant to do it, he would have looked around, he would have remembered the money. She took three small coins and quickly put them in her pocket. She felt a hit of adrenaline, and knew her cheeks had flushed quite pink. She had to hope he didn't know exactly how much he had in coins and that he didn't suddenly rush back in for them. He called again that he was heading to the car, 'Lock the door!' She did, and she skipped down the pathway, her secret money safely in her pocket.

By now his morning moaning was all part of the routine, the bloody this, and bloody that, the damn stupid cyclists, idiot pedestrians, and stupid women drivers. The *bastards* and the *bloody hells*. It started to make Esther giggle. He clocked her in the mirror, so she withdrew her giggle, and adopted a solemn expression as though she was merely considering her lessons for the day.

The car drew up, the lollipop lady was there in her egg yellow and white.

'Well, come on. Get a move on. Get out, you'll make me

late,' he said.

Esther was hesitating with the door, one leg in, one leg out. *Oh… but Ms Butler… and, and, and…* she looked at him hoping he would read her thought and distress and tell her to get back in, that he would drive her to Mum, wherever Mum might be. He didn't.

She stood on the pavement with the lollipop lady coaxing her across the road. She made it to the other side, then hovered, but this wasn't any good. She needed to be seen to be going into school. She had to go to school, for you have to… go to… school. It's the law. Probably.

She smiled and waved goodbye to the lollipop lady who had told her to hurry as she would be 'last in!' And she shot down the side lane as though dashing before that final bell. At the school gates she stopped. A few late mums passed her with their children, then a dad with his little girl, a bit younger than her and timid looking. When they were far enough off she changed direction feeling the comfort of the stolen coins between fingers and thumb in her pocket. She smiled to herself. Just a few sweets, then she would be able to face assembly, stand at the back having arrived late, and then she'd just have to hope the rest of the day would somehow work out fine. Fine, or something… She crossed over to the post office, careful to check for traffic. Mindful in case the white and yellow jacket of the lollipop lady suddenly came into sight. It didn't, and she opened the door of the post office as though entering the home of a very good friend. The man with the beard and spectacles was right where he should be, the mood was calm, the scent of small candies lifted off the air.

Esther chose a few, the accent on strawberry flavoured sweets today. It seemed the day called for an especial level of sweetness. She placed them on the counter without looking up, worried lest the man with the beard scold her for being late to school. He didn't. He didn't speak at all, but simply let his usual gentle aspect filter around the post office. As she placed the coins on the counter, the school bell rang, loud. No mistaking what it was. Esther trembled, the fear of being found out quivering in the air. The man gave her a small amount of smaller change which meant enough for sweets another day. She uttered an almost silent thank you, as though 'speaking quietly' meant she wasn't really there. As she left she added a brief nod meaning goodbye but wasn't sure he noticed. She hoped he didn't think that she was rude.

Outside, Esther took a moment and breathed. She placed a fizzy strawberry sweet in her mouth. Opposite, lay the road to the school gates. The last school bell rang out. There was no one to be seen. No one at all. The lollipop lady had done her duty for now, the kids were at school, the mums and dads had set off back home or to their work. The streets were empty. Whichever way she looked the place was empty. It was as though everyone had left and gone to live on another planet, or everyone had died. Just Esther and the Earth. That was all that was left. Wow. What a strange idea. What a strange feeling! The fizziness of the sweet had passed. It was soft and sticky inside, and something like a small hug.

The post office, just like the school, sat atop a hill. And

when she looked to the right, she could see the long road stretch there out in a perfectly straight line right down to the bottom. Rows of houses to either side. Houses with small windows and identical doors. Houses which looked from the outside as though they would be too small to live in. And at the end of the road, facing it, so to speak, was another road that stretched left to right across it. A wider, main road, where the traffic was faster. And beyond that, the sea.

# 19

Esther checked the street again, there was no one around, so, she turned forty-five degrees to the right and stood at the top of the road taking in the sight before her. The long road down and the perspective was just as she'd seen in paintings with everything narrowing in the distance, and things seeming compressed somehow. The sides of her vision were grey and red-brick brown, the road at the bottom looked narrow though it wasn't, the cars speeding left to right were tiny, like electric toys. The wind suddenly tunnelled up from the sea and made her gasp, her hair made like wings with the breeze beneath them. She giggled nervously, placed another sweet in her mouth, and without further consideration, she began to march down the hill.

She didn't look back. She tried to filter what she heard. Save for the sound of the wind and distant traffic, she must not tune into any voices she might encounter for they could call out her name. And maybe they would stop things.

As she walked, a melody began to form, it seemed in part to be stimulated by her 'strawberry feeling', she smiled and laughed; then becoming momentarily self-conscious, made herself fall quiet, she felt she could hear the sea now, calling.

Without realising how fast she had moved, she was already at the huge road at the bottom of the hill. Everywhere here was open to the full force of the winds, there was grit and dust in the air, she blinked a lot and shook it out of her face.

And she said to herself, inwardly 'don't look back'. It took a while for the traffic to provide a cunning space for her to dart through, but it came and she dashed across. There were railings, she leant forward on them, holding onto the black shiny metal at the top, and she looked out to the harbour across the water. She couldn't see Pete's boat from here, that was in the inner harbour, hidden from view. She thought about her route.

She could walk around the perimeter of the park that lay to the left of the road heading into the port. However, if she did this she would be in plain view of all passing traffic and anyone walking that way, perhaps someone who knew the man or even Mum, since she was beginning to socialise. What to do?

She had never been in the park; she stopped at the entrance. No one around in there it seemed, but that in a sense made her nervous. Parts of the park looked interesting and pretty, but other parts looked dark and woody and forest-like, and... scary. Which way to choose?

The longer route by road, well... ultimately it was just too high risk. She was so very likely to be seen. She took a deep breath and boldly entered the park.

There were voices now, behind her, people heading up the road. She turned and smiled guiltily, about to offer some explanation, despite having none. But the couple passing were deep in conversation and barely noticed her.

She tried to keep her bearings, she couldn't see the sea from here, but it had to be just through there, beyond that thick cluster of trees and shrubs. That was right, had to be...

Sounds to the right. Squirrels. A sound up ahead, a rustling, a dog, followed by a teenager who'd just picked up a ball. He was a boy, he didn't much notice Esther, instead he called to 'Cha Cha' to 'fetch'.

Esther skipped into the trees, her strawberry melody suddenly returning.

So very dark beneath the trees, she stopped to check on the external sounds, that it was only leaves rustling, the boy and the dog in the background. Then she settled back into the music in her mind and hummed along. Suddenly, a man. He had his back to her, just a tall dark shape half hidden by the trees. And a sound. He swung round by thirty degrees, there were droplets. His hands were in front of him as though doing something. Esther ran, scratching her ankles on nettles and thorns, catching her arm on the bark on a tree. She stopped and was suddenly out in the light again. She was on the top of a high wall, perhaps higher than she was tall. Below was a narrow road, and when she looked on she could see how it linked up to the harbour. Perfect. And there it was again, the sea.

But how to get down from the wall? She crouched low and made a rough assessment. Simply jumping the whole way could really hurt and possibly result in a fall at the last moment. She looked along the wall, there were stones sticking out further along. They might not be secure, but if she didn't totally rely on them they might at least offer a momentary foothold to make the jump easier. A car was coming. She let her hair fall over her face. It was gone. She shifted sideways along the wall until she reached a good spot, then aimed for the protruding stones, thinking to somewhat bounce with one foot from one of these and then make the second part of the jump without a break in her movements. It worked, but not without a sprained ankle. She had made the assumption that the stones in the middle would be loose, and that she would somewhat spring off as they gave way, but they were heavily jammed and had not given at all, rendering the first half of the jump a jarring affair.

She crouched on the ground and rubbed her ankle. A car left the harbour, then a minibus but without passengers. She pretended not to look. Then she stood and hobbled her way on the lower road, the one least likely to be used by Mum or the man or any of the other harbour house dwellers, and made her way to the boats.

There was a family on one, 'boat children' she thought, 'boat people' since there were grown-ups too. She stood and chatted. It seemed everyone was on deck. They were shaking things out and airing things like bedding and a rug. There was an older boy, a teenager, practically an adult in Esther's opinion, and a young boy, Robin, who was six. He seemed younger than six, and very sweet. But then Esther knew she seemed older than seven. Uncle Paul had said on the island beach that day that she seemed more like forty! And she had taken this as a rich compliment. So, probably, she would seem entirely like an adult to Robin.

They were friendly, but ever so busy with their chores, so she waved them a hearty goodbye and wandered along. Finally, she reached Pete, moored up but preparing to take a trip out. 'But can I come?'

'Thought you had business elsewhere Mrs?' which was Pete's way of saying 'shouldn't you be at school?' and he glanced at her uniform. Esther pulled at her skirt as though by doing so she could magic it into deck-hand wear.

'Oh, well… no actually.'

'No? Actually?'

'No. Just no.'

'Best you come aboard then.'

Esther was delighted and relieved, and thrilled that this exchange had been so easy, so uncomplicated, and had ended just as she would wish.

'We're going out to sea, mind. And I've no fruit to speak of, though I might have biscuits somewhere…' he went to look in his sailing sack, Esther laughed.

'I'm not hungry. I'll be fine. Are we really setting out to sea?'

'Well, if you stay aboard the next five minutes that will certainly be the case. Best you decide just now, we won't make it back for a wee while, will that do you?'

'It will, Captain!' and she saluted him.

'So then, nowhere else you ought to be? Is that how it is?'

'That's how it is… sir. I am where I ought to be. I'm a sailor after all, aren't I?' and at this she blushed thinking herself too bold. Pete laughed and was tickled. His pipe had gone out, he had placed it to one side and would sort it out once they had set sail.

Esther made herself useful, looking out for obstacles, taking Pete's instructions, on where to be and how to sit and how to stay safe and not fall in.

She hoped he wouldn't quiz her anymore about school or ask about things at home and mostly he didn't. It was as though things were understood. But he did just venture, whilst filling up his pipe, 'No reason then... to be at school, Missy?'

She felt herself go pink again, and hid inside her hair, then she flicked it back and looked up at the sky and offered, 'Too busy Pete. I'm just too busy. Other things to do.' And she hoped that would suffice.

The old man laughed, 'You've projects of your own I expect?'

'That's right, Pete,' and she felt so relieved that this was how it was. That he didn't ask too much, that he placed trust in her without too much explanation, that he let her be. What a good man he was. What a good, good, very good man.

# 20

When Esther arrived back home it was with the natural trep-
idation of having been found out, the fear that her day at sea
was known about, and at the very minimum that her day away
from school had been reported. But the grown-ups had been
busy, and they had a guest. For as soon as Maud mentioned to
her colleague that Esther very much wanted a dog, it tran-
spired that an elderly neighbour they knew could no longer
cope with their four-legged friend, and had been seeking a
good home for her, and the sooner the better. They were all
busy chatting over tea when Esther came in. And though
Esther picked up on the tale of a dog that needed a family,
little did she know, that another guest, the four-legged kind,
was waiting rather thirstily by now in the room next to the
pantry.

The dog's name was Chieko, for the old man who'd owned
her had favoured artists from the East, and Esther was later
told it was best not to change the name, so Chieko it would
be. She was a Collie-Corgi cross, which meant that she had
the build and silky hair of a Collie, the facial cuteness of both,
bizarrely double-jointed hips, and a lively temperament.
Everyone but Maud had quickly agreed that Chieko was perfect for a little girl. 'Well, it might be perfect for Esther, I'm
not so sure it will be perfect for me.'

Esther stood transfixed whilst all of this discussion ran on,
over and around her, coiling round the rims of tea cups, hov-

ering in the pale evening light that dappled the kitchen. She failed however, to fully take it in. Everything just now was quite surreal. Like dreaming. The good things and the bad. Because each thing seemed to dwell in the realm of the extreme. Everything was dislocated, many things were wrong, unfitting, and completely out of rhythm, out of joint. Guilt about the day's events stifled Esther's thoughts. She sniffed at her shirt collar, then her arm. She smelt, and she smelt bad. And then she realised what she smelt of. She smelt of fumes and fuel from the boats, and dead fish since she had later taken a walk by the fisheries, and she smelt of Pete's tobacco too. But Mum, thank heavens, was entirely distracted. This was her opportunity, a slither of time. She had to erase herself from the scene.

'I'd best go change my uniform,' Esther edged herself incrementally from the room, 'I'd best get it in the wash, Mum, ready for next week', and addressing the guest from the doorway, 'Oh, nice to meet you, I'll be back in a just a minute.' Then she cleverly made her exit before Maud could detect anything.

'What a lovely girl,' said the guest. The Man rolled his eyes.

Upstairs, Esther undressed quickly. In one of the pockets of her skirt was a final sweet. She placed it by her bed, pleased by her will power and the thought that she would have something nice should it be needed in the night. She put on her tree-climbing jeans and a long-sleeve T-shirt and skipped back down the stairs, bundling the uniform into the machine as though a helpful gesture. She felt, momentarily, like a murderer, for she had seen part of a TV drama, which she shouldn't have seen, but somehow did, where a man who was a murderer quickly placed his bloodied clothes in the washing machine to 'get rid of evidence'. Blood. DNA. What was DNA? She wondered again if she was a murderer. Then she remembered that she wasn't. She took a very deep breath. Too deep and Mum looked around.

'What?' asked Esther guiltily.

Mum raised an eyebrow, rightly suspecting her and yet feeling there was nothing to go on. 'So, have you gathered what's happening, Esther?'

'Happening?'

The guest chuckled. They had all moved on to wine by now and the man topped up their glasses. They smiled at each other.

'What's going on, Mum?' she enquired gently.

'Though you don't deserve it,' the man jumped in. Esther looked at him as though to communicate that his words came uninvited. He carried on, 'It seems you now have a dog.'

Esther's cheeks flushed, she felt red hot and her ears tingled. Mum noticed and laughed warmly and quickly ran some tap water and gave her a glass. 'Here, have this.'

'A dog?'

'Yes, only like I say, you'll need to do some catching up on good behaviour to earn it,' the man replied, and factoring in the guest, had tempered his words so as not to appear too 'anti-child', he was aware by now, that this was rarely the fashion anymore.

'Your mother will fill you in on all that's expected of you in terms of feeding and care and hygiene; and it can run free in the garden, though not on the dock, and it is not to come inside at all. It has its own room, the one next to the pantry, and when you let it out, it's to go out of the door leading off from that room and not through here. Do you understand?'

The guest was beaming by now and somewhat flushed by too much early evening wine. Esther stepped backwards slowly as though cloud walking and careful not to fall through. The adults were all calling things to her, instructions, a reminder that it was a girl dog, a bitch, that she was called Chieko, and so on, but her thoughts were filled with a strawberry melody and that was all that she could hear.

# 21

Inside Chieko's room it was cold. The walls were stone and not lined in any way. The floor was also stone, and dusty. There was no heating, but it had its own door and it had a window, and so Esther settled to the thought that in essence the dog had her very own house.

Chieko responded to Esther as though they were entirely familiar, almost as if they were already bound one to the other. Licks and gentle jumping up showed a kindness and perceptiveness on the dog's part; she seemed very aware of Esther's size and was careful not to knock her down. Esther found her beautiful.

Since the man had had dogs before, Chieko already had a basket, and Mum had permitted the use of a very old blanket to line it. Mum had then firmly added that if Esther wanted anything more for the dog, she really must ask and not just help herself to things.

Esther was so thrilled by the arrival of Chieko, so astonished that the man had ever suggested it, that he then permitted it, and on top of that, had actually let it happen, that she fell suddenly into what appeared to be uncharacteristic obedience.

It seemed odd also, that the man had said, and so freely, that Chieko could have the run of the garden. He must really like dogs, she decided, adding to her thoughts, *and he must really, really trust me, and… he might even like me after all!*

This was a splendid turn around!

It was Saturday and the morning of Mum's newly titled, 'summer into autumn' 'do'. It was now anticipated that it would mostly likely take place indoors since the eagerly anticipated Indian summer had still failed to arrive. Esther played in the garden with Chieko while the grown-ups attended to grown-up things. It was hard not helping out, in the past Esther and her mum had always been pals and Esther was used to being part of things and on quite an equal footing. It really felt strange to have this ranking enforced, this bizarre separation and hierarchy. Why did being a child suddenly exclude you? Make you incapable of doing things? For you can! Children *can* do things. They aren't idiots. Esther thoroughly disliked the division in status that had, prior to the move, never been part of her life, frankly, not even at school, or at least, not so much. She felt cross about it. Just because the man was an adult didn't make him better. Ms Butler certainly wasn't better. Well… she paused, and knew she had to remember, that at least he'd let her have a dog, and she knew very well that if Mum had remained single, there was no way she'd have let her have a pet. Not so much as a hamster would have been permitted. So, all things considered, she would roll with the situation, and hope that in time the man would realise that she was in fact a person, that she knew things, knew how to do things, and could do some things, rather well. As well even, as an adult.

Out in the autumn sunlight Chieko's gold and white colouring brushed the scene, and Esther's fair hair flowed in smooth, light waves like the curves of the sea in old oriental prints. It sparkled too, with the warm yellow of honeysuckle.

The adults back inside were feeling the tension generated by the thought of 'being on show' to the neighbours, by the hopes that people would mix well, all get along, and enjoy and appreciate the work of their hosts.

After a while, Esther, somewhat grubby, ran inside to get some water. She didn't immediately pick up on the mood. Mum wasn't to be seen, the man was in the kitchen trying to withhold his fury that children had now been included in their planned 'child-free' event. But Maud felt she couldn't simply invite the families on the harbour and not include their children, besides, it seemed ridiculous, it would be the perfect opportunity for Esther to meet them properly and hopefully make more friends.

*But truly, was everything going to be about Esther!*

Mum had stormed off at this point. Very hurt. He knew she had a child when he met her, it was hardly as though she'd hid her in a cupboard and sprung her out after they signed the marriage certificate! 'Except,' he commented, and laughed at his perception of his words as the most insightful wit, 'it wasn't bloody far off!'

'Just getting some water,' Esther offered cheerfully. The man didn't respond. Perhaps he didn't hear, 'Just getting some water for me and Chieko,' she said again whilst hunting for a suitable looking bowl in one of the low cupboards. She found one. Perfect.

He turned on the edge of his heel, 'Is that yours?'

'What?' she said, taken by surprise, 'I mean, pardon…?'

'I said, is that yours?'

'Is what mine?' Esther innocently moved the shallow bowl to the sink and went to turn the tap. He placed his hand firmly over hers to prevent her turning on the water. She gulped a breath, startled and looking up at him, still not understanding. Her question, unvoiced quivered in the narrow space between them.

'For the last time, I ask you, is, that, yours?' and with that he snatched the bowl from her other hand. Then he proceeded, somewhat manically to answer his own question, 'No it's not, is it?' He held the bowl aloft. 'This bowl isn't yours,' he randomly grabbed at things on the draining board and the kitchen table, 'and this isn't yours, and this isn't yours, is it? Well, is it?' He peered over her, she leant back, her arms tucked in to her sides to the elbows, her forearms prone, her hands like the claws of a kestrel, nervously ready to defend.

He drew back, suddenly becoming aware of himself, suddenly choosing adult composure, or so he thought. He took a further step back and made as if to dust himself down, as though to dismiss the last few actions. Esther remained in her startled pose, unsure if strategic moves might soon be called upon.

'So… in future, *in future,* don't just help yourself to things, everything here is mine, and you jolly well ask before you touch things,' and with that he left the room as though his words had been unquestionably reasonable.

It occurred to Esther to cry, but what on earth for, she said to herself. She remembered how Grandad used to say, 'Don't waste tears for no good reason, my sweet. Don't let the baddies see you cry or they'll think they're winning. But the sudden warm memory did draw a tear. *Oh, Grandad...*

# 22

By noon things had calmed somewhat. Some of the man's old pals arrived early. They had travelled far. Esther recognised a few from the wedding day. It was sunny, and they gathered in the conservatory and shared old stories of times living in India and Africa. Esther listened in the hallway, but fearful of being scolded, kept out. She had been told by Mum that it was best to keep Chieko in her room while they had guests as she was likely to jump up a lot in all the excitement, and not everyone likes that. Esther had frowned, so Mum said she would do her hair up for the party if she hurried up and put on her dress.

'Dress?'

'Yes, your pretty bridesmaid dress, darling.'

'But…' Esther still hadn't worked out how to avoid the dress.

'Well, it is a shame not to get some wear out of it, and I thought you liked dressing up…?'

'I…'

And with insufficient resistance it seemed it was decided, and mother and daughter played out a shorter version of the wedding day shenanigans in which too many people had fussed over Esther's 'look' for far too long, and she remembered all too clearly how it ended in vomit. This last part made her giggle.

There were fresh voices downstairs, some of them young. They hurried down to greet them, and the man swung in and took command making formal introductions of the harbour neighbours who were lawyers and bankers, and their children who Esther had seen on the dock but never actually managed to meet. Maud had been surprised and disappointed that the harbour master himself would not be coming, but he excused himself with needing to be 'on duty'. Truth was, he wasn't much for parties.

Of the younger guests, there were brother and sister, Lena and Adam, and the children of the people next door to them, Cara and Rupert. They all shook hands mimicking the behaviour of the adults and giggled somewhat shyly, except for Adam who considered himself more mature. Lena was quite confident and turned to her mother who hadn't recognised Esther without her tree-climbing jeans, 'This is Esther, Mum, do you remember? You thought she was one of the boat children…' and she laughed, knowing that her mother wouldn't want to be reminded, knowing that she would be embarrassed.

Her mother, Sheila, feigned a lack of memory of the matter, leaned over, smiled and shook Esther's hand. Esther was feeling uncomfortable at being overdressed. The two other girls wore nice formal clothes, but knee length skirts and not a silly long dress. Rupert asked her 'Are you getting married?' and scoffed, but Lena and Cara knocked him back quickly, pointing out that he clearly had no idea what a wedding dress looked like.

The man swaggered about now and offered drinks and canapes, 'Let's start with cocktails shall we! I've mixed up some Pimm's for later for the ladies, if they behave,' he laughed, adding, 'and juice for the kids.' Esther rolled her eyes, *if the ladies behaved...???* What on earth did he mean? She shook the thought from her mind, and took it upon herself to give the other children a tour of the garden. She was slightly apprehensive about the duty of keeping them entertained, mostly because they were each one or two years older, and at an age when that year or two can make the most enormous difference. She paused to offer a special talk about the den. Rupert thought the den was 'cool' and admired its construction. Esther blushed, and so Adam took it upon himself to bring things back into line and away from the fuzzy pink heart that had suddenly formed over Rupes, as he called him, and Esther.

'Yeah, right guys, so it's basically a hollowed-out bush. So, anyway,' he paused to run his fingers through his hair, then stood tall with his hands in his pockets. 'Yeah, so, I heard you got a dog, right? So let's see it then.'

'Oh yes, but...' Esther felt conflicted. She wanted to show them Chieko, and she desperately wanted Chieko to have a run in the garden and play with them, but one: Mum had said not to, and two: she didn't really feel comfortable around Adam and his need to take charge, 'it's just that...'

'It's just that what?' Adam made his challenge.

'Maybe the dog's not allowed at the party, Ads,' his sister offered.

'What the hell?' Adam liked to swear, feeling this attached his status more closely to that of an adult.

'Well, it's her bloody dog, isn't it?' He looked at Esther, posturing, and swept his arm upwards as though lightly astounded, 'Well, isn't it?'

Esther chuckled. She'd heard plenty of swear words, mostly on TV when she was meant to have gone to bed and hadn't, and more recently from her sweary stepfather, and she was aware of which age groups used which kinds of swearing. Only super old people like the man said 'bloody', and 'bloody hell'.

Cara had been watching the clouds, and then suddenly shouted, 'Robin! We said we'd fetch Robin! I'll go,' she set off for the gate, then made an abrupt stop and called to Esther, 'Is that alright 'E'?' Cara liked to play with people's names, Adam intervened, 'You can't call her 'E', that's drugs!'

'But you all call me 'C'...'

'Well that's different.'

'I don't mind,' offered Esther, touched by the inclusive feeling of a nickname.

'Well alright,' Cara thought to amend her contraction, 'what about Ess, like an 'S' sound?'

'Cool,' Rupert's reaction made Esther blush again. Adam noticed.

'Oh my god, I mean *p-lease* you two.'

The others all looked at Adam like he was dumb.

'What?' he asked, his hands back in his pockets.

'So, is that OK, Ess, if I get our friend, Robin? He *is* one of the 'boat children' but we just don't tell Mum.'

Esther knew Robin already of course, and thought it a brilliant idea, 'Oh yes, oh yes! And he can meet Chieko too!' She glanced at the others, 'That's my dog.' Having had a little time, she'd decided there was no real reason, no good and proper reason, not to show her dog to her friends.

Cara carried on to the gate, and the rest of them settled to playing hide and seek in the garden until she came back with Robin.

Adam was strangely challenged by Esther and also, deeply intrigued, liking her in a way he hadn't noticed in himself before. He didn't much like how it felt, it was unsettling, and new, and… odd. His sister noticed, and with greater objectivity, seemed to read and understand it. Quietly, when they were standing close by one another, she advised him to stop picking on Esther. He corrected this to 'Ess' as they had agreed to call her, and claimed not to know what she meant.

Cara was soon back with Robin, who was delighted to be included. All the children now ran to Chieko's room, entering through its own special door, knocking first as though they were polite visitors. Chieko jumped high in excitement almost knocking Esther over and then Adam. She jumped and barked and licked them all, welcoming her guests; and then Esther, quite forgetting, swept up in the delights of this brilliant new tribe of friends, ran with Chieko and the others through the garden. She tripped a few times in the dress, but jumped up smiling each time and so they carried on.

Then Adam hatched a plan, he wanted them all to go down the harbour, he wanted to have a 'proper adventure,' and if they were going to form a proper bond and be a club… 'What? What? Well, don't you all want that?' Adam could be very charismatic, and they all found themselves nodding, flattered at the inclusion. 'Then there will have to be some sort of test.'

Rupert piped up, 'Test?' and the girls all looked concerned.

Cara tried to intervene, 'Robin's only six… it wouldn't be fair, Ads.'

'No, no, not like that, not a nasty playground sort of test, er, more like a test of honour, loyalty, like a kind of initiation…'

'Initiation?' queried Lena.

'What does that mean?' asked Robin.

'I was wondering that!' said Cara, now taking Robin's hand to reassure him and smiling sweetly at him.

'Well,' said Adam in an attempt to maintain his position. 'Well, you'll all know it when I think of it. We can head down to where the sand is…'

'We're not allowed there!' Esther asserted.

'That's the whole point, dummy.'

'I mean, it's dangerous…'

'Again, THAT's the point. I mean, like, how can it be? It's just sand.' He went red and clipped the last of his sentence realising that one of the grown-ups, a man called Isaac, had come to round them all up. Get them inside to eat something.

And then Esther's stepfather appeared. He blasted Esther in front of Isaac and the gathered tribe, 'I told you! And your mother told you! Now get that dog and put her back in her room! Now!'

Isaac was quite taken aback and it was clear that Esther's stepfather hadn't seen him, 'Steady on…' Isaac offered gently, and he came from the side and attempted to pat his shoulder only to have his hand shrugged away.

'Oh, yes, yes, sorry, I... *Isaac,* isn't it?' Isaac was a friend of Maud's who hadn't been able to make it to the wedding. Isaac didn't respond, knowing full well that he would surely remember his name having not long since just been introduced.

'Anyway, hurry along now kids, there's food inside,' and with that the man marched on ahead and back inside leaving Isaac with the children. Cara ran to comfort Esther, though Esther was determined not to show signs of needing any. Stupid man. Mean, mean, mean, mean, man.

With her arm outstretched Esther politely gestured they all go in without her while she put Chieko back in her room. She wiped her eyes and sniffed, then skipped and jumped along the way and hummed a strawberry melody. Chieko jumped, and performed what might best be described as a pirouette, and barked her approval.

Back inside the house, and through into the kitchen, voices grew and when Esther finally entered, the room was filled with grown-up bodies, laughing and competing in volume, and smelling of the sweet and sour alcohol, cocktails and bottled ales, and the mixed scent of perfume. There were traces of cigarettes on some people's clothes and exhaled breath. Esther pulled away from those when their faces came near as they bent down low to speak. On the table were the promised jugs of Pimm's, with fruit heavy in the base. Some jugs were almost empty by now, with cucumber strips lining the glass like stray eels, and the strawberries having lost their colour stuck like slugs to the sides.

Esther looked about for the other children hearing their voices in the room beyond, and nearing. The kitchen was difficult to negotiate with so many people. Then suddenly someone called her name, an older adult that she didn't recognise. He began the usual 'Hasn't she grown!' but this she didn't mind, 'Well Esther…' he came towards the large wooden kitchen table which separated them and was home to the jugs of Pimm's. He poured himself a refill. Apparently he was her uncle, Uncle Jeff, but she hadn't seen him since she was three. He lived abroad. 'I was just telling your new dad here…' and he turned and attempted to draw her stepfather into the conversation. The man was busy talking to other guests by now, and offered only a cursory smile as the uncle clapped him on the arm as a gesture of friendship or kinship or some such. Looking back to Esther, and leaning over, the uncle continued 'What a funny thing you are. Like your mother really.' He was drunk. Esther couldn't fathom what he meant. 'I'm just saying, Maud, Maud…' then he pulled his sister into his orbit. 'She's quite an eccentric little thing, isn't she?' He smiled warm and openly at mother and daughter, both he and Maud were still on the other side of the table, and the man had moved yet further back. Esther didn't know what the uncle meant, but it seemed appropriate to smile back. Maud looked unhappy. Esther had no idea how completely dishevelled she was, the dress had grubby green garden marks running across it liked tracks in a field, and her hair was like a bird's nest, a bird not skilled at design. Her cheeks were ruddy and grubby and her lips sat like sweetheart bee stings, wondering whether to impart… anything, or whether to hum to soothe the subtle but evident tension filtering through the room.

Maud went to speak, but lost for words, teared up and held her brother's arm. Esther wondered whether something terrible had happened, but the room was too busy with long tall bodies and it would be super difficult to shuffle through and get near to her. The Pimm's jugs had taken on a mucky hue, the glass sticky with the drying fruit on the insides. Slithers of orange floating like discarded lifebuoys at sea.

'Mum…?' Esther ventured.

'I…'

'A right little scruff bag!' offered Uncle Jeff helpfully.

The man forced his way back to the table behind Maud, 'My god! I mean, my god!' which silenced the entire room. A million eyes, for so it seemed, settled piercingly on the table scene, curiosity nipping the air, pinching Esther's cheeks. 'How is it possible? How is it possible, that a child given so much, can be so readily ungrateful? Um?' The man leaned over from behind his wife, and tearful now, Maud bowed out and left the room.

'Mum!' but Maud had gone.

What was this reaction to? To the dog? But she'd put her back in her room. To her appearance? It seemed a bit much. Surely… She scanned her dress. Bit messy. But… She shrugged her shoulders. She felt her brow grow tense. Hands. Chest. Well, whatever it was, she felt abandoned, and with the lack of true relationship with Uncle Jeff, was unsure that anyone could save things. She tried to spot Isaac.

The room, now entirely silent, seemed to await the next act. Esther didn't speak, so the man continued his tirade, first slugging back the last of a very large brandy. 'So, what in heaven's name have you been doing?'

'Steady on, now,' Jeff attempted to intervene.

'Her mother told me what a *bright* young girl she is,' the man scoffed, 'you wouldn't think it to look at her. But then who can measure the depth of a mother's rose coloured, pebble thick vision when it comes to her offspring,' he seemed to have amused himself again, and went to reward himself with a last slug of brandy only to find the glass empty. Esther chuckled, for it was funny. The man eyed her warily. Jeff fell mysteriously quiet, then he coughed awkwardly, his eyes widening as though attempting to communicate something to his niece, but she couldn't catch his intent.

'Fetch me another, would you?' the man turned to Jeff with his instruction and to Esther's complete amazement, Jeff responded with pure obedience, taking the glass and retreating to find more booze.

'So, what else is there to say, Esther?' By now the other children were huddled distantly between the grown-ups though as close as they could get, curious as to the nature of the scene. They each looked on toward Esther with concern sensing their comrade had run into trouble.

Tipsy, the man leant his hand on the kitchen table to steady himself, 'Esther's started her new school, haven't you?'

Jeff returned with a glass of water, the man looked at it with disdain. Jeff settled it on the table.

'Tell them Esther, how you're getting on at school here.'

What did he mean?

Jeff offered a look of encouragement assuming this would be a tale of some marvellous achievement, for he knew from her mother that she was beyond her years, as she had put it 'by leaps and bounds'.

'I...' Esther's lip trembled.

'Well, let me say it. Esther... Esther, hasn't settled in well...'

What was he doing? 'Look at her. I bought her that dress and all I get... is... is ingratitude and disrespect.'

'That's not true!' she yelped.

'Always some trouble at school and barely even started.'

Jeff seemed to be waiting for some ironic punchline that didn't arrive, and he too furrowed his brow, uttering a feeble 'Uh... I, er...'

'And so, mortifyingly, it would appear that her mother has entirely fictionalised her daughter's 'greatness', since it would seem that her form teacher is recommending she be kept down a year. It's...' and his voice trailed away for dramatic effect, 'an embarrassment.'

Maud had recovered herself sufficiently and was now standing in the doorway. Maud had confided Esther's story to him in confidence. It was private. It was private, and it was utter rubbish that she should be held down a year.

Esther hadn't noticed her mum. She felt a growing pressure from the audience, for so they seemed, to respond. And then suddenly, they were gone. In her mind's eye none of these people were there, she erased them. Instead there was a choir singing, a church organ played, there was sweet almond dust in the air, she inhaled it, and tasted it now upon her lips. But strangely, the man was still there, his arms were raised, moving up and down like a clapped-out machine; the line of his mouth, shutting and opening like tin lids clapping, and nothing but nothing coming out. Teeth like stone, crumbled from within the lines, and fell from his thin tin lips.

As the church organ reached its climax, with the choir holding that vital, neck tingling note in perfect unison, Esther took hold of the nearest jug, still three-quarters full with sticky alcohol and poured it in its entirety, over her head.

*'Esther!'* her mother's voice.

Esther felt brave and proud. The liquid smelt good and somehow comforting. It was sticky on her eyelids, sweet on her lips.

# 23

Esther was lead from the room and Mum took over. She asked what on earth had gone on while she was out of the room, what had she done? Esther sobbed as exhaustion took over. Maud took this for guilt, but was gentle, adopting her 'oh dear me' approach, and undressing Esther for a much-needed bath. But how could she ruin the dress like that? What was she thinking? The marks were mostly grass stains which rarely come out and now there was alcohol too and that was another 'kettle of fish' altogether. Esther stood naked and through her last tired tears called to her mother firmly, deeply, and almost imperceptibly, 'Stop. Please *please*, stop.'

Taken aback, Maud, kneeling on the bathroom mat, did indeed, stop.

'Just no more talking, Mum, OK?'

'OK, dear' she uttered softly in response, 'But…'

'I said *no*,' and with that Esther stepped, sobbing once more, into the hot shallow bath.

She sat in the water, her legs turning red, and wept into her hands.

Completely at a loss for what to do, and feeling she'd best regard Esther's wishes and stop pressing things just now, Maud lay a towel nearby and closing the bathroom door quietly, removed herself.

Esther stopped crying and sat a moment without moving at all, expecting her mother to return, perhaps with an extra towel, some special soap, perhaps having gone downstairs to fetch a glass of water, but she didn't return. She barely washed, but poured some water over herself and lay back to rinse out her hair, forgetting to use shampoo.

She rubbed her hair dry and realised now that Mum really wasn't coming back just now. Not even after all these minutes. She wrapped the large towel about her, and barefoot, took to the landing and listened over the balustrade. There were grown-up voices but none easily distinguished, and she couldn't hear any children, perhaps they had gone home or outside to play again. She sniffed back another tear. The party was still going on but perhaps calming down now, people were starting to say goodbye. Were they all going early she wondered? And was it her fault?

She felt very sad. Nauseous, she made her way to her room, her sanctuary and the comfort of the bed in blue.

# 24

It seemed that Esther was considered precocious, and ungrateful for the gift of the dog, and had in many ways spoilt a family party. The accused was not permitted representation nor allowed to speak on her own behalf. Instead she was sentenced to the expectation of proper and polite behaviour towards adults, especially school teachers, and parents. (You're not my dad, was all she could think.) She was forbidden for the foreseeable future to play out with the neighbours' children and was to consider how she might feel if the dog was returned to its former owner or taken to a rescue centre. To Esther's surprise, Mum did not intervene at all, offering only the occasional, 'Oh, oh…' in some pitying and pitiful tone. What did that mean? It didn't mean anything. It didn't 'do' anything.

When the next school day arrived, Esther woke and started to vomit. Mum soothed her, and rubbing her back suggested, disarmingly, a day at home, telling her not to worry so much about school as she would have a word…

Later when Maud had talked to the school, she explained to Esther gently that she had indeed 'addressed quite a few issues.'

'Issues?' Esther prompted.

'Yes, and now I think you'll find that your teacher, Ms Butler?'

Esther nodded.

'Will be much more understanding. And when you go in tomorrow…'

'To-*what? But…*' Esther knew that a change of heart in Ms Butler, certainly without surgery, was entirely unlikely. 'But, Mum… she… *she…*'

'Don't you worry, my love, it's to be expected that there are a few settling in problems, perhaps on both sides, but I think you'll find they'll adjust at school now and welcome you.'

Flabbergasted didn't even touch Esther's feelings. This was all just so unlikely. Impossible. - OK, it was brilliant that Mum had gone to the school. Had she gone? Maybe she rang them. Ringing was OK… probably. So, that part was fine, but really? Ms Butler, and the school… they were now going to be 'welcoming' and 'adjust'… what did that even mean?

The next morning arrived as though without night to brace it. Esther was out of time. The man was in a rush and they had to go.

'Be polite, Esther, like you usually are, Love,' Mum paused to give Esther a large coin in case she wanted a treat after school and kissed her on the forehead.

Esther wasn't pleased, nor was she convinced, not by any of it. Not for a minute. But she remembered Grandad's words, and took on the expression and self-possession of the invincible, thinking of the heroes of history, as Grandad called them. 'Show no fear,' she chanted to herself inside, just as Grandad had whispered in her ear. And now she could hear her army marching, and claps of thunder resounding in the distance as though to spur them on, as though they owned the rain.

The man regarded her, but this was nothing new. He was aware that she was at times deep inside her own thoughts, and it menaced him. She was strange. Still, best he shake off that thought just now, he had the day to deal with. He walked on ahead. Esther followed with her imaginary army, and the weather at her command.

She settled herself in the car and smiled when she rediscovered the money in her pocket. There was safety all around.

Without knowing quite how she managed it, she found herself at her school desk. She had seen the lollipop lady, had forgone a post office trip, and had walked determinedly, right into that school. She had sung and had listened where appropriate at assembly, and lined up for her classroom. Emma and Rebecca were delighted she was there and one of them held her hand in support. The other whispered, 'I hate Ms Butler,' and the three of them giggled.

But then, part way through the morning, in the middle of the class, something strange happened. The headmaster's secretary knocked at the door of the class taking Ms Butler by surprise. At the door they whispered to one another and the secretary withdrew. The class immediately started to speculate what it could possibly mean, maybe there was a fire! No, they put the alarm on if that happens, maybe there had been a crime, a murder, or something had been stolen. The last idea seemed most likely. Ms Butler closed the door a moment as though protecting someone's privacy and then stoutly called, 'Esther!'

Rows of heads swivelled to glare, most of them astonished.

Esther's cheeks flushed. Emma squeezed Esther's hand under the table and she mouthed, 'It'll be alright.'

'The headmaster wants to see you in his office, and he wants to see you, right now!'

Esther stood up and walked with precise steps, fighting to maintain her composure at least until she made it out of the classroom. What everyone understood without question, was that the only reason that you could possibly be called to the headmaster's office, was if you had done something truly terrible. And more than that, to have the class interrupted, to be called out of class, had to mean it was even worse. Perhaps the police were involved. The air was thick with rumours by the time she reached the classroom door. Ms Butler held it open for her with a wry smile and an unkind eye. Esther ignored her and kept her even pace.

The walk to Mr Jones' office was long. Why did she have to go there? She couldn't possibly have asked for fear of yet more public humiliation. She wanted to wee. Was there time to go? It might look as though she was running away, she must try to hold on. She pulled herself as straight as she could and walked slowly to the office. She wiped her nose on the back of her hand and a few stray tears from her cheeks. She must have done something awful. Just so very awful.

At the door she paused to collect herself, but as she knocked she felt a distinct wobble. Her legs trembling right the way down...

'Come in!' was pronounced from within.

The door handle was stiff. She tried it again, anxiety rising in her chest, her heart skipping a beat, violins played off key and scratched the air.

'Ah, Esther, Esther there you are. Please, do come in.'

It was Mr Jones... Mr Jones the headmaster. He wore a soft grey suit. He was tall and slim, with grey blue eyes. And all Esther could hear were the words, 'Mr Jones, Mr Jones the headmaster', and they seemed to repeat and repeat and repeat.

He talked to the little girl, but she heard not a word of his kind and gentle address, 'So, I hear you've been having a tough time of it my friend. I have spoken with your mum, and she's been telling me what an awful time you've had, especially the experience of being made to stand on a chair, I understand. Terrible. So very, *very* terrible.' He took a moment and then he wondered if Esther had taken this in. She had settled herself right into one of the corners of his office with her arms loosely draped about herself for comfort. Her hair was slightly falling onto her face marginally veiling the colossal tears that now streamed down her face. A wretched sort of sobbing. Sobbing for all the world.

Mr Jones realised this wasn't going at all how he'd expected, how he'd intended. He needed to find a new approach, so he came from behind his desk and squatted down close, but not too close, respectful always of others, of nervous dispositions, of 'personal space', of human peccadillos.

'Esther,' he offered softly, 'I'm not telling you off.' He breathed, worried. 'You do know that I'm not telling you off? And that you haven't done anything wrong, nothing at all,' and he smiled a conciliatory smile, a guilty smile, a smile that wanted to mean so much and seemed just now to mean so little.

But Esther knew, she knew! You are only ever called to the headmaster's office if you are in very big trouble, if you have done something very, *very* wrong. And having assumed the role of the guilty, its weight, heavy on her shoulders, and the pain of being found out, she could not hear a single word he said. For if you were wrong when you couldn't spell, and if you were wrong for not knowing a language, and if you were wrong for moving from one place to live in another, then perhaps you could be wrong for anything, perhaps simply for being.

# 25

Mr Jones' sense of failure from that day would revisit him over and over. He never got to the bottom of it, never truly understood what had happened that day between himself and that tiny little girl. He was so sorry for what she had been through, so pained that it had happened at his school, and he had been so intent on righting the wrong, and yet that day he seemed only to add to a little girl's grief.

She had left his office still in tears, and gone then to the toilets. It was later assumed that she had called her mum to be picked up and had taken the rest of the day at home. But Esther didn't call anyone. Neither did she return to her class, not that day or the next.

She bought sweets, filled her pockets and called them 'supplies', and she marched down the street with the sea straight ahead, dashed through the park, scrambled down the wall, and ran and ran until she found her friend.

'What's up there?' called Pete, 'Not seen you in a while.'

'I thought you'd need my help'

'Oh, I do, I do. Struggling with my radio. They were playing Bach, the French Suites, special favourites of mine, only I can't tune it in now somehow. You up to sorting that out? Know what Bach sounds like? It brings me back to myself somehow.'

'Well I might. I'll do my best.' She started down the ladder, Pete jumped up to steady it.

Inside the cabin, Esther made herself at home. It struck her how clean everywhere was, how it always was, and also how ordered, how tidy.

'Gotta keep it that way, aboard ship,' Pete would say, 'you need to know where everything is, in what condition it's in, in case it needs mending or replacing soon or might run out of batteries, that sort of thing. You can't set sail and not know what you can rely on, you might run into difficulties, even getting stranded is bad enough. I don't have anything on here that isn't of use, and I use everything right up until it's no use at all.'

Esther was most impressed.

She kept moving the dial to try and find Bach. She found some other music but it was pop or jazzy and she felt confident that Bach wasn't jazzy. 'Is this it?' she asked.

'No, no, but seems you're getting close. Keep at it.' Pete climbed back onto the deck. He was searching for his tobacco. 'I've no oranges today,' he called down.

'What's that?'

'No oranges…'

'Oh, oh that's OK. I've got sweets!'

'Oh, sweets. Well, I'll be…' he laughed and knocked his pipe upon the side of the boat. 'And I've got my tobacco! - *That's it, that's it Esther! You found it! Right there!*' He popped his head back into the cabin, his smile as wide as a rocking half-moon, 'What a treasure you are!'

Esther chuckled, 'Really, is this Ba…*chh?*'

'Bach. Yes, m'dear,' adding, oh so softly, 'Listen.'

Pete sat on the top step down to the cabin smoking his pipe and enjoying the music, and Esther listened carefully whilst studying once more the contents of his miniature home. There always seemed to be more things, or different things, each time she looked. On the small pull-out desk she spotted a toast rack, a white ceramic toast rack. And on it lay spectacles, round ones with gold rims, the glass in them sparkled. She chuckled and asked quietly, 'don't you use your toast rack for toast? My grandad does.'

'Pete poked his head down into the cabin again, pulling himself away from the trance induced be the music he adored, 'What's that? Oh, that thing. I'm not one for toast, I have to say. But it makes a fine place to hold my glasses. Always know where they are.'

'I see.' She was tickled by this and impressed at his use of something despite not actually needing it for what it was meant. Clever, she thought.

'Will we go out today? On the sea, later?'

'Not today. Not today...' he answered gently, and it was clear that he wanted to relax and enjoy Bach and probably without interruption, and so she settled herself to enjoying it too. Bach, and the silence, and the rush sometimes of the wind, a seagull calling, and no reply, and distantly, the sea.

Sailors, she thought, we are sailors. And sometimes, this is what sailors do.

# 26

Esther enjoyed the equal terms on which she felt Pete met her. Of course, he knew she was little, but he didn't treat her as little, and he didn't treat her as though she was someone who didn't know how to do things; and if there were things she didn't know how to do, then he didn't treat her as someone who couldn't pick them up quickly. She reflected that this was similar to Grandad.

She wanted to introduce him to Chieko, but she didn't want to sound like a child and so she had left this news awhile so as not be 'showing off'.

'I haven't told you yet, but actually, I've got a dog.'

'Good heavens, you kept that quiet!'

'Well, it's only a dog,' she shrugged, feigning indifference which she thought was what a lot of adults seemed to do.

'But it's a dog. A dog! A new companion.' Pete scratched his head, 'Is it a sailor?'

Without realising at all how funny this would sound, she answered, 'I have yet to ascertain.'

'Oh, I see! And you finished that legal studies course of yours, yet? And your PhD?' Pete laughed with his pipe against his teeth, making a clicking sound.

Esther frowned, then smiled, but didn't catch his meaning.

'So, do I get an introduction then, to said dog?'

'You do. You will, she's called Chieko. It's a name from the East.'

'China…? No, expect it's more likely a Japanese name.'

Esther nodded, 'I think you might be right, Pete, but I'm not entirely sure.'

Esther wanted him to meet Chieko very much, but the dog was very lively and she wasn't certain it would be good to have her on the boat, she jumped about a lot.

'You bring her along when you're ready,' and as though he knew her mind, 'if it turns out she's not so suited to life on the ocean waves, we can always take her for a walk. You got a good lead for her? People are daft round here, letting their dogs run free. All manner of danger for 'em.'

Esther nodded. She didn't know what kind of dangers he meant, but she didn't want to give that away. He probably meant that they might easily fall in the water.

Well, anyway, she always walked Chieko on her lead, despite her pulling and wanting to go free. And since Chieko had the run of the garden much of the time, she had a lot of freedom too. Perfect balance. Esther settled to the opinion that she was a good dog-owner, responsible, thoughtful. Chieko wouldn't drown. She would always keep a close and careful eye on her.

'Oh, you do go deep in thought, dear Esther, don't you? Don't let thoughts settle too long; you should go running, like you do, let the wind sweep them away. You're too young for worries.'

Esther didn't respond. Then she smiled and the two of them sat in silence. Something strangely comfortable for each.

Pete's eyes look teary. Perhaps just from the wind getting up, whistling round the cabin entrance, but his frame seemed sad, and his hands he now held tightly, as though they belonged to two people, one saving, holding on to, another.

'Is something wrong… Pete? You…'

'Did you know the boy? I'm guessing you didn't, that'd be for the best.'

Esther didn't respond. Pete was looking away.

'They not long since identified him…'

'What boy?'

Pete climbed out onto the deck proper and looked out at the mud flats, the water beyond, the sea as it merged with the sky.

Esther followed him.

'In the sand. Last night,' he said, 'I think there were a few of them. All children. By the sand. I worried at first that it was you. God, my heart leapt. But they said it was a boy. Poor, poor dear boy.' Pete stopped talking. The wind got up. They each listened to it, for solace, for a tone that would allow their emotions to settle. Esther thought to ask something, to say something, but it seemed right to allow the wind its breath just now, to permit the sea so far away to breathe over them.

'They think a few of them were playing out late. I was sure that wouldn't be your type of thing,' he looked round at her for reassurance in this. She moved her head from side to side to confirm that 'no' she wasn't there.

'I don't know what you mean, Pete,' she uttered softly, her voice rising on the breeze. She stood in a shiver now the winds were up.

'Last night,' he said again, as though in a daze.

Esther searched her thoughts. At the party Lena and Cara, Ads and Rupert and Robin, they'd talked about the sand. She gulped a breath, 'What happened Pete? Who was it?'

He crouched down and Esther placed her hand gently on his arm, he was distant in his gaze, she looked at him now pleadingly, 'Was it Lena and Adam and them?' Thinking Pete might not know them, that he might not know their names, 'the landlubber's children, the posh ones?'

'It seems it might have been, I couldn't say. All that's known so far is that it was a wee little lad that died... only the grown-ups' version of events so far.'

'*That died...*' Esther tried to see and hold, and feel and unfold this thought. It lifted from her shoulders and then from her arms like feathers, like wings, and swept itself away from her.

'Little lad, Robin, from the boat up there, up the harbour...'

Esther didn't speak, but said inside herself, the little boy's name a hundred times, as though in doing so she'd make him real again, make him breathe again, make him 'be' again.

It seems a bunch of them set off down there to play. Damn fools tried to hollow out a space to sit, like a cave or so, only it seems that Robin stayed when the others had left, or else he went back - they've still to get the story straight. But anyway, however it was, he came to be there on his own, and the sand caved in on top of him.

'Oh no! Oh no!'

'Buried him.'

He held Esther who sobbed profusely, 'I tried to tell them...

'Well, it's a piece of devastating news, but I can't say I'm not relieved that it wasn't you, and I am proud of you for not being there, for having more sense.'

Esther wanted to explain the truth of that: that she couldn't have gone because she wasn't allowed to play with any of those children for a while following events at the party. How despite having warned the others that it was dangerous, she felt that had they invited her along again, she would most likely have gone. These were her new friends, the proper kind, they were a club, a team, a gang, her tribe, and she wanted to do what they wanted to do.

# 27

Back at home, Robin's death was big news. Maud hugged Esther close, but Esther didn't really want that. Mum and the man felt so separate to life on the harbour, and the life of the sea, it was a different world, her world, with her friends on boats, and some in the houses, with the sea and the wind and all the mighty power of nature. Mum and the man belonged in this house where they ate in silence mostly, where there wasn't any music, where she was told not to hum. She could hear Bach's French Suites just now, and she knew right then that Pete had been deeply mournful when she'd arrived. He had been searching for that very music to soothe away his sadness to lift his spirit, to feed his soul. Esther gripped onto her mum suddenly, and Maud felt this as a deep and rich re-engagement with her daughter. Esther gripped so tightly, holding on to the sail in her heart with all her might, lest the wind pick her up and sweep her right away.

'It's not as though she knew that little chap,' the man entered the room, and he thought his tone to be light and warm. The females frowned at him.

'I'm just saying, it's all very well with the histrionics, but seriously…'

'Stop it, please,' Mum took charge, 'Esther's taking this badly. The little boy was one of her friends…'

'But they barely just met!'

And with that Maud fled the room in tears screaming that

in any case it was '*the death of a child, the death of a child!*'

Esther did not look at him, but decided to go and check on Chieko, it was time she was fed. She would tell her the sad news, and then she would sit and console her quietly. Probably, they would both need a hug.

She fell asleep in the dog's room, half curled into the basket with her, half stretched on the cold tiles. Maud wondered how it had been possible to sleep that way. She gently eased her awake, and took her up to bed.


That things such as school life and breakfast rituals still rolled on even when someone had died, completely bemused Esther. It all seemed so wrong. Stupid and stupid and wrong!

'I'm sorry Esther,' started Mum, 'But this is what happens. I'm afraid we do just carry on. We do still eat, we do still go to work and school, and I know, I really do, that it does seem awful.'

'It's not just awful, it's wicked! Robin just died, he just died!'

The man had had his fill, more than. He rose from the table and shook out his newspaper, 'Well, dear, dear, dear, dear, me.'

They looked up at him in unison. They said nothing.

He left the room.


Unfortunately for Esther, the ban on seeing the other children, who were now children who get into dangerous situations, and the ban on playing on the harbour, now clearly the most dangerous place, were both held in place.

Esther stoically went to school, for so it seemed, with Mum packing cake in her lunch box, and giving her some change for sweets after school.

For Maud, the issue of school was dealt with. She had spoken with the headmaster who had been mortified to hear of Esther's experiences, and deeply sympathetic towards the child and the concerns of the mother. He had reassured her that Ms Butler would not only be severely reprimanded but issued with a warning about her conduct, less any further incident occur; and on top of that, he had taken it upon himself to apologise personally to Esther. Maud could not have hoped for more.

Esther suggested that by now she could walk to school, and the man heartily agreed. But Mum thought it too much and too far for her to walk both to and from school. She might find she was really very tired when it came to the end of the day. Both the man and Esther looked at the floor as their united response to this. It always felt particularly awkward to Esther, to feel they might agree on anything at all.

'And besides, you need to walk Chieko when you get home.' Esther nodded and the reminder cheered her, she liked the responsibility of having a dog and she dearly loved her Eastern friend, for so she had come to think of her. Chieko, she said to herself, enjoying the sound.

As the man's car drew up, it was clear that the lollipop lady was suddenly a lollipop man, no matter, but Esther hoped it would not impact on her routine. She eyed him suspiciously, guardedly, as though he might snitch. But what did he know?

Nothing so far. But what if he looked to see which way she went? What if he followed her?

At the school itself, Ms Butler had indeed been served with a warning, and with this in mind she chose not to notice Esther's continued absence. It wouldn't reflect well: she had upset the child so much she had never returned. Best not draw attention to the register. And, if questioned later; she would have made the assumption, she would claim, that the family had moved back to where they came from, or had otherwise 'moved on', though she knew that she would have to be cautious in how she expressed this if called to do so. That Esther did not show her face, caused her immense satisfaction. She had won, and good bloody riddance!

Esther hovered on the pavement longer than usual. It was a mistake as the lollipop man strolled over to ask if she was alright, had she dropped something, forgotten something?

'No I have not' she answered rudely, but she lacked the energy to finesse such things just now, and truly, couldn't he just go away? She did not say that, though for all the world she wanted to.

The man was somewhat concerned, but she walked on, and he put it down to nerves, hers as perhaps a newcomer and his as it was his first day in the job. Still, at least he'd shown concern, and that was good. He popped a dry mint into his mouth and sneezed.

Having waited it out a while, Esther finally peaked from around the side of the old concrete street lamp, and checked that he had gone. Honestly, what was he waiting for? Idiot.

In the post office, she and the man behind the counter moved through their usual silently executed routine as though they had been choreographed. They made their moves with elegance. Esther felt a smile slip from her jaw, but she dared not look up. And did he smile back? She did not know but so it felt.

Down at the harbour there was a police car near Robin's family boat. Esther had wanted to see his parents and his older brother, wanted to say something… wanted to hug them all.

Further along, and what was going on? Pete's boat, gone. Just gone. But…

He hadn't said… why didn't he say… where was he? Where was the boat? She ran and ran, checking the dock in its entirety, perhaps he'd chosen another mooring, perhaps the harbour master had asked him to…

She walked back and across the green to the Harbour Master's Office. She had seen the harbour master many times in the distance, very tall, perhaps in the region of six feet, five inches or so. He was in his mid-fifties. His hair was always windswept, a dark blonde and a slightly darker beard. His face, permanently tanned and lined from the salt winds. His eyes, a pale grey-green. Kind. He looked kind, always looked kind. Esther reminded herself of this. She knocked at the door, then noticed a buzzer and pressed it. She had seen him through the window as she made it up the drive, and there didn't seem to be anyone with him.

The door drew in, 'Hello there! Esther, isn't it?'

'That's right, sir,' she didn't know exactly why she addressed him that way but somehow she felt it appropriate; and she didn't exactly know what a harbour master did, but in her mind it was the grandest role, something in the order of a great ship's captain for a tremendous vessel with a great many sails.

'So what can I do for you?'

'Well, sir… Pete, I'm looking for Pete.'

'Pete? Oh, you mean old Peter,' he stepped out of the door and pointed towards the inner harbour, 'usually moored up down there? The fishing boat?'

'That's right. Only he's gone. The boat has gone.' She looked and sounded so forlorn.

'Oh dear me,' the harbour master looked across now at Robin's family boat and switched his focus, 'you know to stay away from the sand don't you?'

Esther sniffed and nodded. The harbour master turned into the doorway to get something and presented her with a tissue, 'Here…'

'Thank you, sir. Yes, I don't go near the sand. I…'

'That's all right my dear. Listen, Peter, Pete, he sometimes sets to sea for a while. Could be several days, sometimes a few weeks.'

'Weeks?'

'Oh dear, yes. But it's nothing to upset yourself about. He's always lived on his own, likes his own company, and he sets off for some days to… well I don't know what to be honest. It's not my business, but for certain nothing untoward.' He placed a hand upon her shoulder, 'He'll be back soon enough.

I promise, you'll see. He always comes back.' He paused, 'You've got a dog now I've seen. Make sure to keep it on a lead at all times down here…'

'Oh yes, sir. I know that. I mean…yes, of course. I will. I will.'

'I keep telling the dog owners that come down, but most of them seem to let them off at some point. Damn fools.' He smiled at Esther, 'You off home now?'

'That's right sir.'

'You don't have to call me, sir. It's Roger, you can call me Roger.'

'Alright, sir,' and they both smiled.

Esther was disappointed to hear that Pete might have gone away. She wondered why he hadn't told her. She hoped that he was fine. She knew that he was just as sad as she was about the boy, about Robin, oh dear sweet Robin. She wiped her eyes with the tissue and made a small wave to say goodbye to Roger, and wandered back across the green.

# 28

Esther slipped in through the heavy gate, hoping she wasn't seen, and let Chieko into the garden. She went inside and found cheese and breadsticks for a picnic lunch and nestled with Chieko in the den. Chieko was fond of breadsticks, something about the appeal of the crunchy sound as they broke which seemed endlessly surprising, and the novelty of their shape. She often sneezed after biting one from the dry bread particles that fractured before her nose. Esther giggled, 'Silly Chieko, you are such a messy eater.'

After a day of play with breaks to visit Africa and check that all the animals there were fine, Esther nestled back in the den with her favourite blanket and fell into dreaming.

She woke with a start. Chieko was barking frantically and when she gathered herself and sat up to see, the man was coming in through the gate and Chieko was now attacking him. She snapped at his ankles and bit at the hem of his trousers. Esther realised that this was no longer play. She put her hands to her mouth and shook a little. What should she do. The man shouted at Chieko to 'bloody well get off!' and he lashed at her with his brief case and kicked his leg out to the side. It looked so funny at a distance. Esther felt herself blush with the confusion of feelings. She ought to do something, protect the man, stop Chieko biting, but suddenly he kicked her, and she whimpered so that Esther put her hands up to her ears. 'Stop!' she called, and yet she hadn't called out at all. She was dazed by what she saw. Chieko made a last snarl, but when she saw his stance she turned and ran away. He hobbled inside.

Esther had held her breath. What happened now? What happened? She crawled out from her space and brushed off the leaves. She stood and took in the air and let herself grow tall and ran. Chieko was in her room, Esther pushed at the door and the dog looked anxious. She stroked her head and asked if she was alright. 'Wicked man,' she said in a quiet voice. She leant her head against Chieko's.

She didn't understand why Chieko was biting at his ankles, had she done that before? Had *he* done that before, lashed out at her? Kicked her? Her feelings were all jumbled up. Tangled. She was tired. She moved Chieko's water bowl close and promised to come back soon and feed her, then she snuck into the house quietly so as to avoid 'him', and settled in her bedroom for a while in order to think. Mum would be back soon.

She wondered whether to try and tell Mum what had happened, but it would be hard to explain without getting in a muddle and there was so much risk that Mum might find out that she hadn't been to school. And then there was the matter of the man. He switched things around, he might not tell the truth, not how it really was, he'd tell Mum she was making it up.

She thought of Robin. She pictured the sand. She wished that Pete had not gone away on his boat, and she wished she had gone with him.

# 29

In the days that Pete was away, Esther explored the docks further. There was a slate beach at the far reach of the harbour where it met with wasteland. The beach had become home to waste slate from the mines up in the mountains and literally covered the shore in its dull purple shards as though a natural formation, as though it's natural home. Esther stepped carefully across, if you slipped you'd certainly be cut. She placed her feet, watching them as she did so, and taking a breath before the challenge of the next. At the edge of the water she steadied her footing and bent down to find a suitable slate. She skimmed the first on the water with some success, then others failed. But devoting some proper time to this, she soon developed her skill. She would bring Pete here when he came back. Yes. But she couldn't bring Chieko or the jagged slates would cut her paws. Maybe that's what Roger and Pete had meant… not only the possibility of drowning but the danger to dogs of the slates. It was best to take good care.

She let fly her slates across the waters and made wishes and sang songs for Robin. She wanted to listen to Bach again… well, when Pete came back.

And the other children? They were now all kept indoors after school since the little boy's death. Somehow protected and punished, both. But surely, surely later on, she could show them the beach, it wasn't too dangerous, not for children, as long as you took good care. That was it, she would invite them all to purple beach, they would all, all of them together, skim, and they would watch the surface of the water as it danced. As it rippled.

She hummed and then placed a sweet in her mouth. Apples, the world smelt of green, green apples.

The slate beach was not that far from the fisheries, and though the smell made her nauseous she liked to go and peep at what went on there. It was difficult to see, the large doors were never fully open and the windows, though they were big, were too high up. But she sometimes spotted people, the fishery staff in white coats and aprons with white net hats on their heads. They mostly had their heads down moving white trays of fish or placing bands around the claws of crabs and lobsters, all of them brown and red. Well, there wasn't much to be done there, but it had somewhat satisfied her curiosity to feel she knew more about the docks and what went on there.

The drawback of playing too close to the fisheries was that Esther went home with the stench of it on her clothes and in her hair. Mum would sniff at the air and look around and ask rather darkly, 'What's that smell?'

Esther would dash away only to be caught up quickly and be forced to lie about where she had been.

'But I don't understand why your hair smells that way if you've not been near the docks?'

Esther would shrug and look a little hurt at being told that she smelled. Mum, often tired, lacked the energy and suspicion for further investigation and would let it pass, 'But go and have a shower now, eh? Freshen up.'

Esther would nod, and set off the bathroom, relieved at the lack of any real inquisition.

# 30

In the days that followed, Esther was careful to keep Chieko away from the man. That Chieko didn't enter the main part of the house at least afforded her protection, and that she had her own room.

It was lonely without Pete and without the company of the other children. She sometimes spotted them leaving for school or coming back and all waved heartily. It was a deep sad feeling, but surely, very soon, they would all be reunited, and she would lead them all to Purple Beach!

Coming along the harbour, back from her escapades, the wind was up and something about the garden wall seemed strange. A shadow was falling where it did not normally. She regarded it, she stood, stood and thought and she felt anxious but couldn't fathom why. Why? Just the garden wall and the garden gate. It was open, it was open, the big huge gate lay open. She ran and ran, but it would be alright, Chieko was in her room and the door was closed for she had closed it, after her walk, after she was fed. It was closed, it was closed, it would all be alright.

And yet, deep inside herself, she heard no music playing, there wasn't any sound, the world didn't taste of anything at all and there was no colour, there was no colour at all. Salt and sand in the wind as she ran, nothing more.

The gate, wide open. A rock holding it. Open. Esther pushed the rock away and placed her hand upon the gate, feeling it's weight, the grain of the wood… she called out softly, 'Chi-e-ko…' But she didn't know why, for the dog would be in her room. Not able to get out. She ran around the side of the house, there were puddles on the yard but there had been no rain, she observed them for their strangeness, dark pools, like oil, brown, viscose, the light on their surface. She passed them and reached Chieko's door, she pushed it, it wasn't locked. Inside, no dog. She gulped some air, turned and ran, calling out her name all around the garden, then racing up and around the docks, calling to everyone, had anyone seen her dog. She ran to the harbour master's to see if he knew anything but he wasn't there. It seemed as though no one was there, anywhere.

Her throat dry, her body aching, she made it back to the garden. No grown-ups around, no one to ask. She should be at school but cared nothing now to be found out, she had to find the dog!

She searched about the garden again, the den! It was the most obvious place and yet she had left it out. Chieko whimpered from beneath the trees, Esther squatted down and called to her gently to draw her out. Was she hurt? Esther leant forward. Chieko was laying there, shaking uncontrollably. Esther placed her hand upon Chieko's hip, it was damp, she withdrew it. Blood. It was blood, rich dark blood. The pools in the yard… she gasped and screamed Chieko's name. Screamed and screamed. She ran outside the garden again to look for help. Oh, where, oh where, was Pete? She needed him the most. Stupid sailing! Then *Roger*, she spotted him, tall and lean strolling up close to his office. She ran and crashed into his legs, he tried to break the impact of collision and gently but firmly held her shoulders, squatting down.

'She's dying! I think she's dying! My dog… she's got blood…'

'Oh, dear god… where, Esther?'

Esther pointed to the house and the two ran back. She was entirely out of breath, Roger patted her on the back and crouched down to see what state the dog was in. His hand too, immediately bore her blood. 'She must have been out of the garden. Has she?'

'The gate was open when I came back, but I had locked her in her room, I know I did!' She wept, 'Will she be OK?'

He turned to her, his hand on her arm, 'It's not your fault,' and then more firmly, 'it's not your fault. Look, I'll fetch a vet, that's the best thing to do here. We'd best not move her right now. Do you want to come and phone with me or stay with Chieko?'

'I'd best stay,' she said, and they nodded agreement.

When the vet came, he wanted the dog moving, and struggled to lift and then carry her to her room. She was weak, shaking, and there was so much blood, dark, red-brown, pooled and spattered everywhere it seemed. The vet focussed on her middle, her stomach, her intestines.

Roger stood over next to Esther while the vet examined her.

'Was I, right?' Roger enquired. Esther looked up at him,

unaware he had a theory.

'Yes, it looks that way, I'm afraid,' the vet answered. He was called Mr Thomas, and Esther regarded him. 'We'll need to do something right away. The pain…' Mr Thomas grimaced, as though he sensed the scene unbearable. It was.

'Will she be alright though? Can you do something? Make her better?'

The two grown men withered. What to say?

Roger squatted down again, 'It's the warfarin, Esther…'

Esther didn't know what that was. She looked at him questioningly and then at Mr Thomas.

'Are her parents about?' Mr Thomas asked.

Roger and Esther shook their heads.

'Is it alright if we do this Esther, I don't want her to be in all this pain?'

Mr Thomas pulled a syringe from his bag and some other small things.

Roger took over the explanation while Mr Thomas prepared the syringe. 'Esther, it's the fisheries. Recently they started to put down warfarin, though I tried my best to talk them out of it and even tried to involve the Council…' he knew that he was rambling.

'What's warfarin?' she asked in exasperation.

'They've a huge problem with rats you see. It's got a lot worse of late. Warfarin, it's poison. It looks as though Chieko must have eaten some…'

'But she'll be alright?' she pointed to the syringe, 'You'll give her some medicine then she'll be alright?'

Mr Thomas took over, 'Esther,' he squeezed her hand, 'We all have to be super brave now, can you do that with us. Just so very, very brave. Chieko's in an awful lot of pain, and we can't make her better. I wish that I could.'

Tears streamed down her face. Mr Thomas took a breath. Roger wiped his eyes.

'But if I give her this injection, it will make it easier for her, more comfortable, take all the pain away.'

Esther nodded that she understood.

'But we can't make her better. We can just help her to sleep now. Will that be alright?

Roger spoke up, 'It's the kind thing to do. She won't last, my dear, but we can make it easier for her just to fall asleep.'

Esther understood more than they realised, 'So she'll go to sleep now. But she won't wake up. Only sleep now, for now and always?'

'That's right,' answered the vet.

'So, she'll be dead, she'll be dead?'

The men both nodded, hugely uncomfortable.

'So, do it. Do it now!'

Mr Thomas was startled, Roger attempted to encourage her to stand back but her will was certain. 'I want to see, I want to stay with her,' she rightly anticipated being asked to leave the room. 'I won't leave, I'm staying, I'm staying right here with her, till the end!' She moved around to the back of the basket and placed her arms gently around the dog. The men admired her bravery. Roger stood back, the vet did what he had to do.

'Esther, will your Mum be back soon?' he checked his watch. She nodded. The vet had to leave but left his card with Roger, and Roger had to get back to his office but promised to come back as soon as he could, would she be alright? Again, she nodded. Then just before he left she asked, 'What's his name?'

'The vet?'

'The boss, the man in charge at the fisheries?'

'Brian Brooks…' Roger looked at her quizzically. Esther let her gaze fall.

'I'll be back as soon as I can,' and with that Roger departed.

Roger couldn't make it back quite as soon as he would have liked; Esther coiled herself around her dog, comforting her and then she slept. When she woke, Chieko had passed away. Her limbs were heavy, her head a weight in the small girl's hands. She kissed her muzzle and her forehead and stroked her fur.

She wiped the tears from her face with her hands and stood up straight. Her shirt and skirt were drenched in blood.

She closed the door to Chieko's room and marched down the harbour. Somehow it reminded her of her first time there, though this time she wasn't running. She needed to be strong. She needed to conserve her energy. But she didn't notice a thing as she moved towards the end of the dock, she heard nothing, felt nothing, focussed only on the pace of her feet.

When she arrived at the fisheries, she took hold of the sliding door and pushed with all her might. The staff, all in white, looked around. She stepped inside and demanded, 'Where is he?'

'Who you looking for, Love?' came a response from a young man who smiled at her. They began to eye her blood sodden clothes. Her steely determination cooling the air.

'Brian, Brian Brooks. Mr Brian Brooks.'

'The owner?'

'The owner.'

She stood between two stone lobster ponds, for so they seemed, two bricks high, lobsters with their claws held in rubber bands, shuffling about. Not getting anywhere.

The young man looked to an older woman for approval, she nodded and he ran to fetch his boss. When Mr Brooks came from the floor above and walked the length of the room, the staff paused in their work again, readying themselves for what might come. Mr Brooks seemed amused that a scruffy little girl was demanding to see him.

'Can I help you?' he asked warmly. He smiled. The staff giggled, but Esther looked around at them and they halted.

'Brian Brooks. Are you, Brian Brooks?'

'I am.'

'The owner of all of this,' she gestured with her hands.

'That's right.' It was the strangest of scenes. He observed the blood on her clothes, dried now and brown.

He squatted down before her aware that his staff were watching his every move.

'You killed my dog!' She let out brokenly, the tears welling up inside.

'I what?' he asked gently.

'She said you killed her dog!' said the young man accusingly.

The tension grew.

Then someone added, 'It'll be the warfarin.' and several others 'Ayed' in agreement.

'The warfarin…' said Mr Brooks quietly.

'You, you, you killed my dog…' and she wept aloud.

Mr Brooks attempted to put his arm around her but she shrugged him off, he went to explain about the rats, but she'd already heard about the rats, already understood…and so what!?

'YOU KILLED MY DOG!' she screamed from the pit of her stomach.

There was nothing he could say, she turned and ran. She forgot that Pete had gone away and dashed to the inner harbour, he wasn't there, *he wasn't there*, not back, and why wasn't he there? Oh why?

Shuffling her feet back home she sat on the steps by the gate. Roger came by, he'd heard what had happened at the fisheries, Mr Brooks was very, very sorry, did she want him to explain everything to her mum?

'I don't care, I don't care! Do what you want!' and she ran inside. She lay by Zebra awhile and slept.

# 31

Mum agreed that there should be a funeral. The man wanted to curtail any expense, he would dig the hole and they would bury the dog in the garden. It could be done very nicely. 'You can make a special cake or something, whatever it is people do.'

Esther told them both to stop calling her 'the dog', her name was 'Chieko', and that she didn't want a bastard cake. Though the 'bastard' part caught her by surprise, she'd never said it out loud and wasn't entirely sure how she'd chosen it, but it was out and at least it had sounded powerful. The man ignored her and complained instead about the vet bill, and so it was agreed that it would be best from now on, to let the issue of pets, of owning any, keeping any, or even rescuing any, to rest for once and for all. A lot of expense at the end of the day, and a lot of distress one way and another. How did he do that? How did he manage to make his selfishness seem as though he cared. Esther knew that Mum had reacted to the word 'distress' and allowed herself to believe that his meanness was actually him trying to protect her from further loss and disappointment. Bastard, Esther said to herself. Bastard, bloody bastard. A quiet fury burning inside.

*And how was it that gate had been wedged open? Who did that? Hey!* Esther knew you shouldn't blindly accuse… she couldn't be sure.

Esther had stopped looking for Pete. She couldn't bear that he wasn't there, and she couldn't allow the thought that he might not come back enter into her mind. Instead she played in the park and down on Purple Beach, and sometimes on other people's boats.

After the man and Esther had set off as usual, as though heading to school for the day, a letter arrived from Esther's school. Esther had been absent some weeks by now and without explanation.

It was of course a week day, but Maud had booked some days off. She wanted some 'me' time: salons, shopping, siestas. There'd been such a lot to cope with lately. She read the letter over and over in perfect disbelief. Not at school. For some weeks. Esther. And so… if Esther wasn't at school, wasn't turning up… where in hell's name was she?

Half a glass of red wine. Maud's hands were shaking. Where had she been if she hadn't been going to school? Where was she going every day? For weeks! Weeks? Her mind raced. She gulped the wine and immediately wished she hadn't, yet poured some more. So, where oh where had she been going? She thought back to the smells on Esther's clothes…

Her husband drove her to school. Dropped her off each day. Didn't he? And so? And…

There was a knock at the door. She hurried, opened it. An old man stood before her, somewhat bedraggled, wellington boots. 'You must be 'Mum'?' he said cheerfully.

'I must?'

'Esther's mum,' he said emphatically.

'I am… yes. And you?'

He put out his hand to shake hers. She hesitated.

'I'm Pete. Esther's friend, Pete. Only I've been away and Roger just told me the sad news about Chieko…'

'Chieko?'

'Esther's dog.'

'You know my Esther and Esther's dog?'

'That's right.'

'And you are?'

'Pete, Esther's friend, Pete.'

Maud waivered. What had he said? This man? The stranger before her. The soft spoken old chap. That he was Esther's friend? He knew her, was her friend? Knew her dog…

'You alright, there?' he interrupted her thoughts with his gentle tone.

What to say? What to say… show anger, dismay, not show anything, not give away that she did not know his name, his existence, the friendship. The friendship? What was that? Roger, Roger must know, have known, and he did not mention… What the hell was going on?

'Pete?' she enquired, as though, what? *As though what?* She was buying time, saying his name as though it would imply quite the right thing that ought to be said. So what ought be said?

'I think I'm interrupting you, or taken you unawares perhaps,' he said, sensing her discomfort, 'best I let you be, perhaps come back later. Well… if you wouldn't mind? If you wouldn't… mind… might that be best?' He was somewhat puzzled now. For surely the woman would know him, of him, his name at least?

'She's missing,' said Maud, 'I got a letter, from her school. And she's missing.'

How could it be, that such a short summer and a step into autumn could so shape a little life?

# 32

Despite herself, her anger with Pete for being away so very long, and not even having said goodbye, Esther had decided to check the inner harbour once again. He had to know he'd been away now far too long. Surely he would realise, would know, would sense on the breeze that it was time to come back, that he was needed. Even so, she braced herself for the disappointing vision of an empty mooring once again, and worse than that, the very real possibility that there might be another vessel moored up where Pete's should be.

Too long to be away, so very much too long – she tried to remind herself not to wallow for it made things worse and things of late had been entirely bad, and entirely sad. So, enough. She exhaled.

Danger and sadness everywhere, perhaps everywhere in the whole wide world.

The badness had to stop. And life, just like the sea, had to have its tides, didn't it? Sometimes in, sometimes out, sometimes low, sometimes high... wouldn't Pete say that? She began to pick up her pace, forgetting how the last part should go, and slowly the rhythm of her step changed the rhythm of her mind – sometimes high, and sometimes higher – she looked up into the skies, and out upon the seas. To the seagulls and the winds. The dark wisps of cloud streaking the sky. The cawing way above, the rumbling of distant rain clouds heavy with their burden about to sweep in. And the sky grew black.

But the boat was there, it truly was there, settled in the harbour, right where it was meant to be.

And later, grief gathering and hovering in the mist, Pete and Maud would find her there. Sleeping. In a bunk inside the cabin. Cradled by the sea.

# Acknowledgements

To my publisher and editor at Seren, Mick Felton, thank you so much for all the sensitive work involved, a light touch requires so much more than people might imagine and you are deeply appreciated. And to all the Seren team, thank you so very much for all that you do.

I must give special thanks to Mark Thomas, you are like a brother to me. To Katie Manning, thank you for being such a dear friend, and for rescuing me from my laptop crisis. Often-times it seems the writer cannot afford the tools.